Annie O'Neil spent most of her childhood with her leg draped over the family rocking chair and a book in her hand. Novels, baking, and writing too much teenage angst poetry ate up most of her youth. Now Annie splits her time between corralling her husband into helping her with their cows, baking, reading, barrel racing (not really!) and spending some very happy hours at her computer, writing.

Also by Annie O'Neil

The Doctor's Marriage for a Month
A Return, a Reunion, a Wedding
Making Christmas Special Again
Risking Her Heart on the Single Dad
The Vet's Secret Son
Christmas Under the Northern Lights

Double Miracle
at St Nicolino's Hospital collection

A Family Made in Rome
Reawakened by the Italian Surgeon
by Scarlet Wilson

Available now

Discover more at millsandboon.co.uk.

A FAMILY MADE IN ROME

ANNIE O'NEIL

MILLS & BOON

First published in Great Britain 2021
by Mills & Boon, an imprint of HarperCollins*Publishers* Ltd,
1 London Bridge Street, London, SE1 9GF

www.harpercollins.co.uk

HarperCollins*Publishers*
1st Floor, Watermarque Building,
Ringsend Road, Dublin 4, Ireland

Large Print edition 2021

A Family Made in Rome © 2021 Annie O'Neil

ISBN: 978-0-263-28805-6

10/21

MIX
Paper from
responsible sources
FSC
www.fsc.org   **FSC® C007454**

This book is produced from independently certified FSC™ paper to ensure responsible forest management. For more information visit www.harpercollins.co.uk/green.

Printed and bound in the UK using 100% Renewable Electricity at CPI Group (UK) Ltd, Croydon, CR0 4YY

This is to the doctors
who dedicate themselves to the
advancement of medicine, helping
women and children everywhere.
Thank you.

CHAPTER ONE

'HERE WE ARE.'

Leon's lips brushed against Lizzy's neck, his familiar touch and lightly accented voice sweeping through her nervous system like the New Year's Eve fireworks display they'd just slipped away from. Dangerous. Dazzling. Powerful enough to unearth a thousand memories she'd barely managed to stuff into a box over the years since they'd seen each other last.

She tried to sweep them away again, desperate to believe that the past didn't matter. That this chance meeting wasn't fate forcing her hand, demanding that Lizzy confess to Leon he was the only man she'd ever loved. An admission that would definitely send him running back to the seven hills of Rome.

It had been five years since their paths had last crossed. Hardly a surprise, considering she worked in Sydney and he worked in Rome, and their lives—professional and personal—had never intertwined as they had once before here in New York during their surgical internships.

Not one email. Not one phone call. No texts. Nothing.

But she still knew him well enough to know that telling him she loved him would put an immediate halt to whatever was about to happen behind this hotel room door. And, God help her, she wanted to go into that room. She wanted him.

He ran his fingertips along her bare collarbone. It was all she could do to contain a low groan.

Of all the medical conferences, in all the world…he'd had to walk into hers.

He stroked her arm and a skittering of goosebumps added wattage to the flames already burning bright for him. When she realised the touch had been accidental—that his hand had been on the way to his pocket to check for his key—her body's automatic heated response offered a new perspective.

Perhaps the sentiment she'd been clinging to these last five years hadn't been love at all. Their shared passion for antenatal surgery, their mutual desire to be the best, the head-to-head competition their mentors had encouraged, pitting them one against the other to be the very best, and their obvious physical attraction... Perhaps all those things added up to nothing more than good old-fashioned lust.

It wasn't as if she wanted to sit and talk to him about feelings all night long. Or their pasts. Those types of moments had never defined what she—perhaps wrongly—had called their relationship.

What she'd felt for him then was remarkably similar to her response to him now. It was primal. Instinctive. An animal attraction. A shared hunger for the same goals in life colliding at the perfect time and place. The only difference being that last time they'd had two years together, while this time they had one solitary night...

Her body was responding to him as strongly as it had the first time they'd met. Crackling and sparking as if the seven years since that moment had never existed.

But they had. And ever since they'd both left New York there had been a part of Lizzy that believed their relationship might have been something more if only they'd given it the oxygen to breathe.

In fairness, she'd been as marriage-shy as he

had. Not that she'd ever told him why. Who wanted to unload a mountain of childhood misery into a relationship that was fuelled by a shared belief that the world of antenatal surgery was theirs to conquer?

But now their individually built, hard-earned professional futures had led them here, to the most elite medical conference in their field. Where, once again, they were being drawn to one another like a moth to a flame.

But who was who in this scenario?

She definitely didn't want to be the moth. No way was she going to let a night with Leon consume the self-respect she'd built for herself after her move to Sydney. She'd beaten herself up for years for letting herself fall in love with him back then, despite a silent vow to keep things simple. No more moth behaviour for her.

No. Tonight she wanted to be the flame. Wanted this to be the night she finally understood that the energy they shared was purely physical. Was being with Leon tonight the best way to make those years of self-doubt disappear? Who knew? But she was tired of living on an emotional rollercoaster—being yanked this way and that, wondering if she had lost her one chance at happiness.

Maybe they were more similar than she thought. Two moths. Two flames. Neither of them willing to admit to feelings that were too frightening. Too raw. Or maybe they just fancied the pants off one another. And—wouldn't you know it?—there was a fancy hotel room waiting to help them out...

Her eyes drifted to the hotel room door, willing it to give her a nudge in the right direction.

Honeymoon Suite

Leon had seen her taking in the gold script on the door. Their eyes met and meshed with an intensity that blazed through her like wildfire. It had been a long time since she'd felt like this. Out of control. So she did the only thing she could think of to regain that control.

She snorted.

There were many things she believed were going to happen behind that closed door tonight, but consummating a marriage neither of them wanted wasn't one of them.

'Upgrade.'

Leon's shoulders hitched into one of those shrugs of his that spoke of countless similar upgrades. It wasn't vanity, or a limitless bank account, or his natural charisma that swept people under his spell. It was what Lizzy had used to playfully call 'The Cassanetti Effect'. She'd certainly not been immune. For two near-perfect years. Perfect right up until the end…when it wasn't.

Leon cupped her chin for a kiss she'd not yet let him take.

'Uh-uh.' She smiled and pushed him away from her.

Not too hard and definitely not too far. Arm's length. A safe enough distance for her to regain control. She was determined not to let him steal her heart for another five years. The next five hours, though… Could she allow herself one perfect night of passion and then walk away from whatever it was they shared once and for all?

She made an impatient noise, edging herself away from a tumultuous trip down memory lane.

C'mon, Lizzy. Get a grip. This is lust, pure and simple.

Sure, she'd been blindsided when she'd seen Leon surrounded by a crowd of admirers at the conference's celebration dinner. Her body had felt as though it had disappeared, leaving only untamed energy humming in the centre of the room where she'd stood. And a thousand emotions had collided into one vital sensation: desire.

Seeing the one man she'd thought she'd never see again had felt heady and frightening and thrilling all at once. An energy too powerful to dismiss.

But she'd tried to pull herself back into her body. Remind herself that tonight was about her career. That the only reason she was here was because she was the keynote speaker. Her focus and dedication to her career had paid dividends and, as such, feeling tingly because her ex-boyfriend was here was ridiculous.

He'd extricated himself from the group of people he'd been speaking to and crossed the room with the determination of a man who'd found the Holy Grail. He'd taken her hand in his and wordlessly lifted it to his lips.

His name, when she'd said it, had tasted like warm caramel on her tongue, without a trace of the bitterness she'd thought she might experience if she ever saw him again. And then, as if the years they'd spent apart had been swept away by an invisible hand, Lizzy and Leon had become inseparable, as if leaving one another's side wasn't a physical possibility.

They hadn't spent the time catching up, exactly. There hadn't been any need beyond her glimpse at his ring finger—which was still, unsurprisingly, bare. Just as her own was. She'd read about his work in medical journals and presumed he'd done the same about hers. Only a few people in the world dealt with the types of cases they did—which, she supposed, made it completely insane that she hadn't expected to see him here.

After half listening to their peers for a spell, their hands occasionally brushing, eyes catching, the energy between them had inched ever upwards towards the moment when, without speaking, they'd eased away from the crowd, his fingers weaving through hers as naturally as they had that first time they'd sneaked into an on-call room and confirmed what they'd both known for several months.

They wanted one another.

Tonight was no different. He wanted her as much as she wanted him. It was the perfect opportunity to tie a nice shiny bow on the end of five years of wondering *what if...?*

The answers lay just out of reach.

After one, possibly two orgasms, and a bit of a cuddle, she would have fulfilled her animal desire and then she could set herself free of Leon Cassanetti once and for all.

Another shiver of goosebumps swept across her midriff as his hand slipped along her hip, his fingers grazing the cut-out in the fabric that laid her skin bare just at that magic spot where waist began to swoop into hip. She couldn't stop a small sigh of satisfaction.

Again their eyes met, and a slightly more fevered quest for that missing room key got underway.

She took advantage of the moment to really look at him.

Leon Cassanetti.

The man who broke the mould.

She allowed her heart one careless flip and then realigned her focus. This wasn't about spiralling back into an out-of-control, unrequited love dungeon. This was about closure.

Well…

Pleasure and closure.

The two could co-exist, right?

Maybe they cancelled one another out.

Of *course* they could co-exist, Lizzy assured herself slightly desperately. She wanted to feel that unbridled joy she'd felt when they were together just one more time. One night of hot hotel sex didn't have to mean reopening the scars of heartache. No matter what her father said, she was a modern woman. A modern woman, with modern needs, who'd felt like a modern-day Cinderella from the moment her eyes had met and cinched with Leon's a few hours ago.

But unlike Cinderella she wouldn't spend her days in the scullery, wondering if Prince Charming was going to show up at her door with that damned glass slipper. Just like last time, he'd get on a plane to Rome and she'd get on a plane to Sydney. Only this time she'd walk away first. Eyes wide open.

It was just after midnight now.

A symbolic moment to mark the beginning of a new era.

She glanced at the closed door again. Once they went in, there would be no turning back.

She caught him looking at her inquisitively. As if he'd seen the flicker of hesitation in her eyes and was leaving the final decision as to whether or not they went in up to her.

Was there still enough magic in the air to let this be the final chapter of their story? Give her the closure she so desperately needed? When she looked into his eyes she saw nothing but longing—a hunger that gripped him with the same intensity with which her love for him had held her to ransom all these years.

His desire was intoxicating. A stark reminder of why impressing other men hadn't mattered to her over the past few years. Because of this man there was a string of failed first dates and briskly wrapped up mini-relationships trailing behind her as long as a kite tail.

She'd never admit it to anyone, but that moment five years ago when he'd turned and gone had made her feel as if he'd ripped her heart out of her chest and taken it with him. It was her own fault, really. For letting herself believe emotions could be flicked on and off like a light switch. She'd had her reasons for wanting to keep her feelings for him under control, but the one thing she'd failed to do was tamp down that flicker of hope that he might ask her to join him in Rome. The hope that had flickered right up until he hadn't.

Now, here they were—five years later, a little older, a little wiser. As she'd planned, she had climbed the ranks and now had a great job as an antenatal surgeon in Sydney. She was a leader in her field, actually. That was what happened when all your unspent love and energy got poured into your work. And Leon had just taken the helm at the antenatal unit in Rome's most prestigious children's hospital, which suggested he'd possibly done the same. Worked to fill the void left by the relationship that had nourished them both.

She forced her gaze to turn clinical. Tricky, when she had the urge to tuck her finger into his belt buckle and tug him towards her as decisively as she'd pushed him away. He was more handsome than she remembered. Extraordinary, given the fact that merely thinking of him had the power to turn her insides molten.

His dark hair still fell in soft, gorgeous waves, lightly grazing his eyebrows and, more sexily, his shirt collar. It wasn't pitch-black, like many Romans' hair—a rare mention of his father had unearthed the fact that he was half-Scandinavian. His eyes, though, were pure Italian. As dark brown as the shots of espresso he'd always favoured when the alarm went off at an ungodly hour and they'd headed to the showers, pulled on fresh scrubs and begun another day at the hospital. His smile, often hard-won, might have been its own solar system.

At thirty-seven he was still young and vital,

but there was a new, decisive aura of 'proper man' about him—as her father had used to call the men he'd admired. Those who took charge. Held the reins. Told women what they did and didn't want from them and stuck to it.

Leon brandished the key with a smile.

She masked her darker memories with her own smile, but she wasn't entirely sure it reached her eyes. Tonight wasn't about fulfilling her father's outdated beliefs that anything a woman did was fuelled by emotion, and that men were required to fulfil their duty and, as a result, could treat the women in their lives however they felt. Tonight was about closure. Full. Stop.

She felt her lips quirk as she gave the mental image of herself and Leon at a flower-laden altar a casual flick into an imaginary bin. She replaced it with a steamier image, her breath catching in her throat as it gained traction.

Leon took a half-step closer, his hands resting softly on her hips. He looked at her expectantly, his dark eyes scanning her features for any sort of tell.

'Lizzy? Are you sure? We don't have to do this.'

There were countless answers to the seemingly simple question. *Yes. No. Rip my clothes off, already.* But Lizzy didn't bother answering, choosing to let her gut do the deciding. Actions spoke louder than words, so she took the newly unearthed key card out of his hand and held it against the electronic lock before she could change her mind.

It flashed green and the door clicked open.

His full lips curved into a smile. He'd never disguised his pleasure when she took the lead, and this was a blatant show of her desire.

Yes. She wanted him. Had done for the five years they'd been apart. Well, the four years, eleven months and eighteen days. No need to get hysterical.

The small of her back grew warm and tingly at his touch as he held open the door and guided her into the suite. The bright lights of Manhattan twinkled like stardust out beyond the twentieth-floor bedroom, giving the space an even more magical hue. As if they needed any external razzle-dazzle to increase the sparks that were flaring more and more with each passing moment.

Leon stood behind her as she feigned an interest in the view. She was actually staring at his reflection in the window. This was hello and goodbye to the ghost that had stayed with her for far too long.

She shivered as his fingers teased her shoulder-blade-length hair away from her neck, so that he could drop a few sensual butterfly kisses upon her skin. She felt his lips hover above her shoulder, where the thin strap of her dress held the lightest of purchase.

As if he'd rehearsed the move a thousand times, he slipped both straps off her shoulders so that the dress skimmed down over her goose-bumps until it puddled onto the floor around her feet. Soon enough there was skin upon skin, heated breath matching heated breath, and kisses so deep and powerful the rest of the world faded away.

Yes. She'd made the right decision. For now the world was Leon. When morning came she'd get up, give his cheek a farewell kiss, and bid *addio* to this man who had held her heart captive for much longer than he deserved.

CHAPTER TWO

Three months later

'Dottore Cassanetti?'

Leon blinked at the foetal echocardiogram he'd been staring at for quite some time. Prompted yet again, he looked across at the nurse who, judging by her slightly impatient expression, had clearly been trying to get his attention for a while.

He gave the high-tech screen a tap. 'Tough one, this, Constanza,' he said, meaning it.

Foetal surgery was never easy. In utero surgery on one half of a twenty-six-week foetal heart ratcheted the difficulty up to a level only a few antenatal cardiologists in the world could handle.

He was one of them. The only other one he'd trust was half a world away.

As if on cue, his eyes played the same trick they had been playing on him ever since he'd left New York… A cloud of straw-blonde hair briefly appeared just beyond Constanza's shoulder and along with it a soft hint of floral perfume. But every time he went to check if it was really her there was, of course, no one there.

He cleared his throat and forced himself to focus again. He'd earned his place among the elite in paediatric medicine the old-fashioned way: by pouring every fibre of his being into his work.

From a young age his mother had drilled the importance of self-reliance and the fallibility of love into his psyche. Relationships didn't last. Professions did. She'd led by example, dedicating every fibre of her own being to her job at an art gallery when her relationship with his father had fallen apart.

Thus cautioned, and unwilling to endure the years of grief and bitterness that had become part of his mother's cell structure, he'd planned his future with meticulous care. University in England. Medical School at Harvard. Surgical internship at Columbia in New York City, gaining as many contacts as possible before returning here to Rome, his beloved home city, to practise at St Nicolino's—one of the most prestigious paediatric hospitals in the world.

Its historic stone edifice belied what it was inside: a high-tech epicentre of medical excellence that attracted some of the most complicated cases from across the globe. They were a fiercely passionate bunch here at St Nicolino's, united by a shared love of pre, ante and post-natal healthcare.

The day he'd been made head of the antenatal unit had been one of the proudest in his life. What could be better than leading a massive team of medical specialists who gave mothers and yet to be born babies a proper shot at living a full and healthy life?

Having someone to share it with?

He shook the thought away. He wasn't built for relationships.

His conscience knocked him on the head.

Okay. Fine. Perhaps that wasn't entirely true. Seeing Lizzy again had thrown a thousand barbed questions at an ethos that had, up until now, always worked for him. *Work hard. Play at your own risk.*

Apart from during his internship in New York, when he'd come as close to having a proper relationship as he ever had, work had always been his lifeblood. It was the only way to avoid the type of pain his mother had endured when his father left them almost thirty years ago.

Leon had been unceremoniously sent to spend a summer with him once in Denmark, but his father had made it very clear that he wasn't regarded as family. The blunt reality was that he hadn't even acknowledged his presence. Not with one solitary smile.

He'd not returned to Denmark since, incising the pain of that visit with the same surgical precision he used on a daily basis. Neat. Clean. Permanent. As such, he had a reputation for going where other surgeons suggested caution. He performed procedures other specialists only read about. But since the New York trip he'd added a new and unwelcome string to his bow. He was now the only elite maternal and foetal specialist in the world who spent his spare time daydreaming about making love with a woman he'd likely never see again.

Lizzy Beckley.

Allowing her name precious headspace inadvertently gave it access to prowl through the rest of his body. Trying to push it back into the box he'd kept it in these past few years didn't work any more. It was as if chaining it up and then unleashing it for that one perfect night had only magnified its power.

Her name sounded silently again, reverberating from his head to his heart, warming his chest and then spiralling further down, producing darts of heat that expertly arrowed below the drawstring waistband of his scrubs.

She'd been on fire that night. They both had. It had been as if everything that had ever transpired in the world had happened so that he and Lizzy could share those few rarefied hours of lovemaking. He'd never felt more connected to one person in his life.

When he'd awoken, she'd gone.

He'd felt the sting of her absence so sharply he'd struggled to draw a complete breath since.

Constanza's fingers drummed impatiently on her hips. There was also a foot-tap.

He gave the echocardiogram a final thorough examination to flush his system of inappropriate thoughts. A child's future was reliant on his unerring focus. He'd have to stop this. The daydreaming. It didn't do him any good, and nor would it change the fact that Lizzy had made it very clear she had moved on. He had to respect that. Even if it was driving him insane.

'If you could head down to the imaging lab...?' Constanza persisted, not unkindly.

She was clearly used to doctors being lost in their thoughts. Perhaps not the precise strain of thoughts Leon was having right now, but suffice it to say the woman was made of patience.

Leon followed her down the corridor towards a part of the ward he knew perfectly well. He'd spent countless hours in the imaging lab, poring over X-rays, echocardiograms and ultrasounds, ensuring his plans were in as perfect condition as possible before he began the complicated surgeries he regularly performed.

Constanza had fulfilled her name's meaning—constancy—during one of the hospital's most complicated times. In those Covid-19 days, when life and death had hung in a balance more precarious than any of them had ever experienced bar Constanza, who came from a war-torn African country. She said she'd looked a real enemy in the eye and lived. She wouldn't let an invisible one take her down either.

Seeing families separated at the most painful and vulnerable times imaginable because of fear of the virus had made him grateful he didn't have a family of his own to worry about...children's futures to fear for. He saved lives on a daily basis in tandem with his incredible team here at St Nicolino's, and when his work was done he went home to his clean, quiet sanctuary to recharge for another day of pushing the medical envelope.

He was, in short, a man who had fulfilled his mother's dreams for him. She'd ensured that her son relied on no one, because she believed it was easier that way. If you relied on someone, you'd only be let down. If you needed to indulge in a bit of male-female relations you must cut it down when you knew you could still walk away.

Unsurprisingly, it had been his mother who'd been the most bemused by his choice of medical specialty. Paediatrics. Why would he want to spend his life around something he'd never wanted? she'd asked. Children? Families?

He'd always laughed it off, but since she'd passed away a few months back going home to his empty flat after a day with pregnant mothers, anxious fathers and the newly delivered babies that magically turned a couple into a family had pushed him into an occasional uncomfortable moment of self-examination. One that went beyond what he'd been forced to see when his mother had died without a lover or a spouse by her side.

He'd felt only a hollowness since her death—not missing her, because she'd never given him enough access to her for him to truly feel a loss. The hollowness was more of an ache. A black hole that had opened up inside him, aching to be filled with light.

He knew exactly whose light he'd like to fill it.

Lizzy's.

How the hell he'd walked away from his most perfect relationship—his *only* relationship, really—was beyond him. Youth, he supposed. Naiveté. He hadn't really trusted that Lizzy would hold up her end of their unspoken agreement to walk away at the end of their internships, without remorse or tears, and yet she'd done it. Wished him well, boarded her plane, got on with her life...

If anything, he was the one who'd stumbled. Not back then. He'd been too blinkered back then. But seeing her again had made him wonder...

Holding her. Touching her. Feeling his body rejuvenated by her warm floral scent...

He'd thought he'd be able to walk away from that solitary night refreshed and charged for another intense, head-down assault on his surgical skills, but for the first time ever one night hadn't been enough. Not nearly enough. And he wasn't entirely sure what to do with that.

'Dr Lombardi is waiting,' said the nurse, in a way that suggested she was repeating herself. *Again.*

Giovanni Lombardi was one of the most respected surgeons he'd ever had the privilege of working with and he was lucky to call him a colleague. Widowed four years ago, he had a gorgeous little girl—Sofia—whom the entire hospital seemed to dote upon, and none more so than Giovanni himself, whose world largely revolved around her and his work.

Saying that, the man was never short of female attention. Whether or not any of it stuck Leon had no clue. He intentionally kept himself clear of post-op banter as it always ended up circling back to him and his own very distinct lack of a social life. It was a frailty in some of his colleagues' eyes. A strength in his own. Especially when the boss was waiting…

'*Si.* Of course. *Scusi*, Constanza. I—' He made a vague gesture with his hand for which he received an eye-roll.

He'd received a bounty of those over the past few weeks—as if a memo had been circulated around the hospital announcing that Dr Cassanetti was a few scalpels short of a surgical set so everyone should be on their guard. Which, of course, was unacceptable. He needed all his synapses firing. Particularly with this new case Giovanni Lombardi was waiting to share with him.

An hour later he was buzzing with adrenaline, his concentration crystal-clear. Giovanni had presented him with a once-in-a-lifetime opportunity: foetal surgery on conjoined twins. The list of complications was as long as his arm, but he'd have the freedom to build his own medical team to ensure things were done properly. More to the point, he was going to have the chance to help two little girls live normal, healthy and, with any luck, happy lives.

Giovanni ran through the case again, more quickly this time.

Conjoined identical twins with two near-perfect hearts. Early scans had suggested they were hugging. The twenty-week scans had shown otherwise. Now, at twenty-one weeks, having had much more detailed MRIs, advanced imagery had made it clear that the little girls shared one crucial aortic valve. Baby A, as she was presently called, also appeared to have hypo-plastic left heart syndrome.

Long story short: if Baby A survived the pregnancy she'd endure a lifetime of hospital care unless there was a surgical intervention.

There were other complications. The girls shared a chest wall, the lining of the heart and a liver. These were largely surmountable prob-lems for when the separation surgery hap-pened—Giovanni's responsibility—but the mother's health, the babies' delivery and Baby A's left heart syndrome was Leon's focus.

As a maternal foetal medicine specialist he was best placed to oversee the mother and the babies' welfare until the children were born. He could, of course, do general foetal surgery if required, but he'd need a foetal cardiologist as part of his team. The mother and her babies would need monitoring throughout the dura-tion of the pregnancy and, of course, during delivery, at which point Giovanni and his team would assume pole position in overseeing their health and, ultimately, the separation operation.

The mother, Gabrielle Bianchi, was twenty-eight years old and five months pregnant. Only married six months, this was her first pregnancy. She was scared, Giovanni cautioned, but having been referred by a trusted doctor in her native Switzerland, she and her husband were hopeful that their baby girls would live through their ordeal. Her husband would be staying in a nearby flat, owned by the hospital, whilst Gabrielle would stay here in St Nicolino's for monitoring.

Leon pored over the complex medical notes again. When he glanced up, Giovanni was looking him square in the eye.

'You sure you're up for this?'

'Never been more sure.'

'Only a couple of hospitals in the world have even attempted this.'

Leon grinned. 'What? And that's meant to intimidate me?'

'No.' Giovanni gave the back of his neck a scrub. 'I just—I'll want your complete focus on this. You know as well as I do it'll end up being much more complicated than those notes suggest.'

Leon nodded. 'I get that, but…' He tipped his head to the side, his eyes still on Giovanni. 'You've never been worried about my concentration before.'

'I've never had to be before.'

That got his attention.

Leon pushed his chair back from the table, acutely aware of his temperature rising as his defences rushed to the fore. He pushed the paperwork to the centre of the table as if it were a prize only one of them could win.

'There's not been a solitary mistake made in my operating theatre.'

'I know, but you don't seem—' Giovanni stopped himself and sought a better word than the one he had clearly been about to use.

Whatever people said about Giovanni—that he was a charmer with the gift of the gab— he was a brilliant Chief of Surgery. He never played the 'Me Boss, You Underling' card. He fostered teamwork in a way that didn't always happen naturally in high-pressured, big-ego-filled hospitals like their own, where half the medicine practised was the stuff of science fiction novels.

This case would be no different. They'd pull in the 3D printers, the lasers, the robotics. Everything they had, they'd use. Not for show. But because the type of medicine they practised here at St Nicolino's was ground-breaking. Not by force, as Leon always explained to people who didn't know about their work. It was more organic. In the way a microscopic seed could grow into a beautiful plant or tree right in the middle of a city. The wildflowers that made a show every year at Rome's ancient Colosseum were testament to that.

He squared himself up to his boss. 'C'mon. Out with it.'

Giovanni wrote an invisible prescription on the table with his finger before answering. 'It's nothing you've done, per se, but ever since you've got back from New York I haven't been able to tap into that Cassanetti drive that assures me you and your team will be able to go where no paediatric hospital has gone before. It's not a slight. Your work has been flawless. But there's been *something*…something I can't put my finger on.'

Leon raised his eyebrows. 'Oh?'

Giovanni gave him a look. One that indicated he knew damn straight that Leon could tell him here and now what the problem was if he wanted to.

He was right.

The problem was about sixty-five inches of feminine wiles, with hair as soft as silk, skin to match, and a brain that put most mortal's to shame. Never mind off-the-charts surgical skills. But Leon wasn't really in the mood for opening up a Lonely Hearts Club Forum.

Giovanni rose and pushed the paperwork back across the table towards Leon. 'You know as well as I do that your work has been exemplary. I'm just saying if there's something going on in your private life that is sapping your focus...kill it, fix it, or put a plaster on it until this is over. For the next three months your life is all about the Bianchi twins. If you want it to be.'

'Oh, I want it to be.' Leon didn't need to think about that.

'Right answer.' Giovanni reached across the table and shook his hand. 'You're the one surgeon I know who will put together a team that will make these girls' lives a reality.'

Putting together a team...

A command to fix whatever it was that was distracting him...

An idea hit. It was mad, but...

Screw it. You only live once.

'I can bring in anyone?'

Giovanni nodded. 'It's going to be a high-profile case for us. We don't just want the parents fighting for their daughters' lives. We want them to know we've got the entire world crossing their fingers for them. And you know how I feel about crossed fingers.'

Leon laughed. 'Not necessary if you've got a St Nicolino's team on it.'

They shared a grin.

Leon hitched his fingers onto his hips and feigned a casual air he didn't quite feel. 'Have you heard of Dr Elizabeth Beckley?'

Giovanni looked out of the window to where the winter sun was setting in a late-afternoon fanfare of oranges and reds, lighting up the Vatican City on the far side of the river as if by celestial arrangement.

'Antenatal cardiologist, I'm guessing. British?'

'Australian,' Leon explained. 'One of the best. Antenatal cardiologist, though she's performed a wide variety of antenatal surgeries across a pretty impressive spectrum of specialties. I'd like to bring her in.'

'For the HLH surgery? Great.'

'No,' Leon corrected. 'For the rest of the pregnancy.'

There were valid reasons for having a cardiologist on hand throughout the pregnancy. One stent might not do the trick. The twins were joined at the chest and they shared that crucial aortic valve. There were any number of problems that might arise that would require a neonatal cardiologist beyond the HLHS. But having this particular cardiologist here for the duration would be expensive.

Giovanni's eyebrows shot up, but he said nothing. He was used to surgeons and their big asks, and this was definitely one of them.

'No one here would be suitable? We do have paediatric cardiologists who live a bit closer to home...'

Leon took the question on the chin. He could see that Giovanni was asking a bigger question here. Would Lizzy solve his little concentration problem or make it worse?

Professionally, of course there were a smattering of surgeons who could do the surgery. Any who could solve the other problem...? Not so much.

'She and I interned together in New York.'

That was as close as he was going to get to crying on Giovanni's shoulder and telling him that he'd once had a love life and what had happened was his own damn fault.

Giovanni gave him a slow nod of dawning understanding. 'Get me the paperwork and we'll make it happen.'

And just like that Leon felt the so-called Cassanetti Spark pour back into his system.

CHAPTER THREE

A SMILEY FACE.

Lizzy gave the stick a shake, almost willing it to turn into a frown. Nope. Still smiling. Why hadn't she gone for the one with lines instead? The smiley face felt so…personal. Lines were scientific. Anonymous. Not bright, shiny portents for a future that was suddenly a thousand times more complicated than hers had been three minutes ago.

She leant her head against the cool tiling of the hospital loo wall, willing it to calm the heated storm brewing in every corner of her body. The tiny tempests preparing to surge together to force her to accept what this little stick had already understood very clearly.

She was going to have a baby.

And not just any baby.

She was having Leon Cassanetti's child.

While the pragmatics of a surprise pregnancy didn't entirely elude her—women often experienced bleeding that seemed like a period, wrote off other symptoms as tummy trouble or working too hard, until—as had happened today—all the little dots began to connect together into a smiley face.

Her brain fuzzed and whirred and countless futures danced in front of her like film previews, each inviting her to dive in and explore. Not one of them involved a smiley face. None she would let herself believe in anyway.

Leon was... *Oh, man.* He was a thousand things and none of them all at once. Brilliant. Passionate. Driven. Devoted to his work in a way she'd never seen in any surgeon before or since those two remarkable years in New York. A commitment-phobe. Didn't want children. Didn't want a family. Didn't want her.

But...

Even with all those factors digging little knives into her heart, one thought persisted.

This is your chance.

She'd never let the thought crystallise until now, but somewhere buried deep inside her was a hunger to give a child the kind of carefree, deeply loving, innocent upbringing she'd never enjoyed. A future primed with possibility and hope and, yes, some cautionary notes, but not enough to make her—or him—as shy of relationships as she was.

It wasn't as if Leon was completely to blame for not falling head over heels for her, asking her to marry him and move to Rome, where the pair of them would live happily ever after, their lives full of surgical triumphs, lovemaking and, as they'd be in Rome, a lot of incredible gelato.

No. She'd fallen in love with the one man in the universe who was absolutely perfect for her apart from the fact he didn't love her. He'd had his chance. That ridiculous night when she'd told him she loved him.

To this day she still wasn't a hundred percent certain he'd even heard her. It had been in a busy bar in the middle of Manhattan at the end of their internships. The tequila had been flowing and everyone had been hugging and exchanging addresses and promising to stay in touch. Like a fool, she'd leant towards the man she'd spent the last two years with—either in the operating theatre or in a bed—and said, *'I love you.'* Nothing more. Nothing less. He'd said nothing, so she'd pretended she'd said nothing.

She'd tell him, of course. About the pregnancy. She had to. Morals. Ethics. Honesty. The triumvirate of principles she clung to in her professional life were stalwarts in her personal life too. Such as it was. Yes. She would tell him. But she'd also be very, very clear… Neither she nor this child would interfere in his life. The only thing she would ask was that his child be able to contact him. She'd like their child to hear it straight from the source why Daddy and Mummy were living separate lives.

Her hand flew, for the first time, to her belly. The protective gesture spoke volumes. She would do whatever it took to ensure Leon Cassanetti never hurt her child the way he'd hurt her—unwittingly or not.

A couple of hours and a lot of regrouping later, Lizzy was standing outside the NICU unit looking at all the tiny lives she'd helped bring into the world when a nurse ran up to her with one of the mobile phones they kept at Reception. Unusual… Normally they took messages.

'It's a call for you about a job.'

Her eyebrows went up. Good! 'A job' was always code for something difficult, and difficult meant she could temporarily keep her mind off the fact she'd be having a baby in six months' time.

'In Italy,' the nurse whispered, the way one might say *chocolate cake*.

Lizzy's hand was shaking as she took the phone.

'Lizzy?'

Her entire body hummed with nerves as she stood and listened to Leon as he told her about the conjoined twins, the shared aortic valve, the baby with HLHS, and said that he'd be honoured if she'd join him in Rome for the next three months.

'Sure,' she said.

She wasn't capable of saying anything more. Not on the phone. Not when so much was at stake. Not when she knew that the next three months would decide, once and for all, the kind of life her child would lead.

'Leon! Great to see you! Whoa! No need for two cheek-kisses— Oops... Oh, well...when in Rome...'

That was a little over the top, but in for a penny...

Arch an eyebrow. Pause. Wait for his response.

'What? Me? No, I look dreadful. Jet lag doesn't suit my complexion. Leon, listen...' Lizzy let her features rearrange themselves into the expression she knew her patients saw when the news was serious. 'I've got something important to share right off the bat and I'm not going to beat around the bush. I'm pregnant. It's yours. Just under three months—*obviously*—so that does mean no flying after a while. Which leads me to logistics. I'm still very keen to play my role with the twins—*thank you*, by the way, for including me on the team. A real honour... Seriously... But as soon as we safely deliver them I'll be moving back to Australia.'

Pause. Nod. Furrow brow.

'Yes, permanently. I'm sure you'll agree it's for the best seeing as a girlfriend let alone children aren't really on your radar, so—'

She watched her mirrored expression falter and then crumple into the confused, strained mess it had been ever since she'd first stared at that positive pregnancy test.

The fact that Leon's call had come two hours later had shaken a thousand shards of 'not a coincidence' into her bloodstream. Her hands pressed one over the other on her stomach. Why did this have to be Leon Cassanetti's baby? The one man she'd tried and failed to wash out of her hair countless times? So much for her stupid one night of unbridled passion wrapping up that chapter of her life. Now she was going to have to start writing an entirely new book. One with a baby in it.

She cleared her throat and tried to push a bit of confidence through her spine. The man was probably nothing more than a handful of metres away from her right now, so she had to get her act together.

Leon had been nothing less than professional on the call, so she knew her place on his team was solely about the conjoined twins, the boost to his hospital's profile and, with any luck, her own—although a boost in professional stature wasn't why she'd agreed to come. Obviously there was a part of her that had said yes out of professional curiosity. But, more crucially, she was here to ensure her child knew where it stood with regard to its father.

Someone to keep at bay for ever? Or someone who wanted to play a role in his or her life? Doubtful, but—unlike Leon—she knew what it was like to have a father in her life, and even though her own father had definitely not set the bar very high she wasn't going to deny her child access, if that was what the two of them wanted.

She stared at herself, wondering how the hell she'd got herself into this predicament. The two people in the world least equipped to have a baby were having a baby.

If she ever had sex again, the man would have to wear three condoms. Four. Maybe she'd just never have sex again...

Outside the loo she'd locked herself in, she heard the tannoy. The voice was Italian, obviously, and as a result sounded sensual and impassioned with a splash of urgency thrown in. Italian, except when spoken during lovemaking, always sounded as if it were laced with urgency.

The soft, cadenced murmurs of appreciation Leon had whispered into her ear as they had made love at the dawn of the New Year came back to her as viscerally as if he was there with her now, tracing his fingers along the downy soft skin on her cheek, her arms, her belly—

Right. Hashing over the past wasn't helping anything. Not that sleeping with her ex to get over him had been a particularly brilliant idea either, but what was done was done. The strawberry-sized baby in her belly wasn't going to be well served by hiding here in the ladies' room.

She jogged in place for a second, trying to loosen a reminder of why telling him in person had seemed such a good idea.

Because it's the right thing to do, Lizzy.

She tried to marry her conscience with her frazzled nerves, fixing her reflection with a bright, cheery smile only to watch it morph into a frown. No amount of rehearsing was going to make this any easier. It was rip-the-plaster-off time.

She gave her shoulders a little shake, pinched some colour into her cheeks and forced herself down the corridor.

A few moments later she stood in the door-frame of his office, her body buzzing as if she had one hand on an electric wire and the other on a jackhammer.

He was engrossed in something he was reading on the latest model tablet, looking every bit the Grade-A surgical specialist he'd set out to be in med school. His office was filled with high-tech screens, a pair of stylish yet comfortable-looking leather chairs, a sleek espresso machine—of course—and little else. No old-fashioned piles of paperwork in this hospital.

His hair was a bit longer than when she'd seen it last. His stubble more a 'nearly midnight' shadow than a five o'clock one. She must have got the highly groomed version of Leon on New Year's Eve. This one was a bit more...not free-range, exactly... Maybe feral?

There had always been an animal element about him she couldn't quite define. An attractive animal element. The poised, tightly controlled sensuality of a tiger on the prowl. How every woman in the world he met didn't swoon and leave her partner and beg him to be with her for ever was a bit beyond her, but—given what she was about to tell him—it would very possibly remain one of life's eternal mysteries.

She forced herself to knock on his door. 'Leon?'

He turned and saw her, his eyes flaring with something hotter than recognition.

'Lizzy. *Come stai?*'

He leapt up from his chair, his long legs diminishing the space between them in nanoseconds. His scent enveloped her as he lightly held her by the shoulders and doled out the obligatory Italian cheek-kisses, instantly rendering the pink she'd brought to them with a couple of pinches pointless. Vanilla and something spicy. Whatever it was, it smelt edible.

He held her out at arm's length. 'I was just about to send out a search party.'

Ha-ha.

'No need for that. Here I am.'

Me and your baby.

'Was the flight all right?'

He peered at her as if he truly cared. Her heart constricted in a way it wasn't meant to. *Did* he actually care? It was an angle she hadn't actively considered. Then again…he always looked as if he cared, no matter the secrets he was hiding.

'I'll always think of you with fondness…'

Okay, he was 'fond' of her—which was the kind of feeling you had for spinster aunties, which meant he genuinely was asking about her comfort on the flight.

She considered making a crack about the lack of peanuts taking it down a notch, but knew it would be petty and a delaying tactic not worth pursuing, considering a) the professional reason she was here, and b) the personal reason she was here.

So, instead of playing Let's Engage in Meaningless Chitchat, she skipped all the niceties and forced herself to voice the real reason she'd come.

'I'm pregnant.'

He shook his head in one short sharp move. As if she'd slapped him.

'Scusi?'

Remorse washed through her at the coarseness of her reveal. It wasn't the way she'd have liked to find out that an ex she'd had a one-night stand with was changing her life for ever. Was there even a good way? She didn't know. This was new to her, too. Even so, she heard herself pour apologies into the charged empty space between them.

'Sorry, I—I didn't mean it to be so blunt. I was going to soften the blow—'

His eyes eventually refocused, peering into hers, actively seeking answers to the logjam of questions she presumed were stuck in his throat.

'It's mine?' he asked eventually.

She nodded, her cheeks flaming an even deeper red—because if he'd known anything about her life these past few years he'd know the chances of her being pregnant by anyone else were pretty slim.

'But we—'

She nodded. Yes. They had used protection. His, in fact.

He went completely still. An intense motion-lessness so powerful it felt as though an invisible, impenetrable energy field had surrounded him. It frightened her to the point that she actually dropped her eyes to his chest to ensure he was still breathing.

When she looked back up he still hadn't

moved, but she could see his eyes darting back and forth, as if he was watching the denouement of a thriller. The moment when the true mastermind of a horrible plot to take over the world was revealed. In this case, she supposed it was her.

He was fact-checking her story, no doubt. She felt herself being swept into the journey he must be reliving. His face had softened. Was he remembering the moment when they'd been able to wait no longer? They'd been in bed, not a scrap of clothing between them. She'd already orgasmed, thanks to the luxurious amount of time he'd taken to reacquaint himself with her body's erogenous zones—as if their one-night surprise reunion was actually the beginning of a long journey they'd be taking together. With a groan of sheer longing, he'd grabbed his wallet, pulled out a little foil-wrapped packet...

He shook his head as if he was trying to let the facts settle into a new order. One in which he either did or did not make room for her.

'Come,' he said eventually, his closed-lipped smile warm but distracted. 'You must be exhausted. Why don't I introduce you to the team and then we can get you to your hotel for some rest? Then we start fresh tomorrow, *si*? The twins' parents are coming in at nine. We'll be keeping *mamma* in from there on out.'

He wasn't even going to acknowledge it?

Gosh.

Of all the responses she'd prepared herself for, this definitely wasn't one of them. Anger, joy, confusion… She'd had those bases covered. But full-on denial? Definitely not a reaction the Leon she'd thought she knew would have. He might not be the down-on-bended-knee-with-a-sparkling-ring-to-hand type, but he was a kind man. An honourable man. At least…that was what she'd thought.

She was forced to swallow the bitterest of pills. The Leon she'd thought she knew was a fiction. A man she'd let herself fall deeper and deeper in love with the longer they were apart. This moment was proof that she didn't know the real Leon at all.

Somewhere along the way she'd rewritten their New York internships into a fantasy of burgeoning love, when what it had actually been was two headstrong, horny, trainee surgeons having a brilliant time competing and bettering themselves at work and releasing their pent-up tensions in bed. And that had been that.

They'd both had provisional job offers in other

countries well before their internships were over. Neither had ever offered to move to the other's country. Oh, she'd dropped a hint or two, but Leon had never picked them up. Deliberately ignored them, maybe. As he was ignoring the fact she'd just told him she was pregnant with their child.

She'd been a fool to think the chemistry they'd shared had been love. More of a fool to believe that one more night of lovemaking would lay it all to rest.

In a daze, she went through the motions. Smiling. Shaking hands. Laughing as the staff congratulated Lizzy on her halting Italian.

She wouldn't dare admit that she'd spent her first couple of years back in Sydney studying all the medical lingo she'd thought she might need when Leon rang her, admitted he'd made a mistake and invited her to move to Italy. The call had never come. And, not wanting to shame herself by begging for just a morsel of attention, as her mother had so often done, Lizzy had done her best to step away from her dreams of being reunited. She'd put them away in a cupboard, shuttered her mind to the fantasy of a bright, sexy, surgical future together, and let her Italian become dusty and lacking in fluidity with disuse.

Mercifully, despite the discord she could feel buzzing between her and Leon, the staff made her feel welcome, and she knew working here would be more pleasure than pain. If she didn't board a plane back to Sydney tonight…

When they'd finished the tour and found themselves alone again, Leon looked at her as he might any visiting doctor. Politely.

He held up his phone. 'I'll just let my team know I'll be out while I drop you.'

Wow. It looked as if they really weren't going to talk about it.

Wait.

He was going to drive her to her hotel?

Her brain reeled to make the necessary connections and came up short. The exhaustion she'd held at bay with nervous energy suddenly swept into place. Her limbs felt leaden and her clear, pre-prepared thoughts were fogged with fatigue. Sitting in a close space with Leon Cassanetti, her version of kryptonite, when she felt so vulnerable was definitely a bad idea. She didn't have the right kind of energy to do this. Not on her terms anyway.

'A taxi will be fine,' she spluttered. 'You don't have to—'

'Yes.' Leon cut her protest short. 'I do have to. You're a guest here. At my hospital. In my city. And,' he added, finally taking ownership of the child she had convinced herself he was preparing to deny, 'there is no chance I'm having the mother of my child wandering round Rome unescorted.'

A niggle of discomfort cinched round her heart. From one angle, his choice of words might be seen as protective. Kind and thoughtful—just as she remembered him. They were the words of a man who was going to step up. Accept the shared responsibilities of the child neither of them had expected. From another it was bordering on controlling. A childhood of living with someone who valued strength over compromise meant she didn't respond well to being controlled with alpha power. She wasn't sure she liked the way the conversation was going.

'C'mon, Lizzy.' He beckoned for her to follow him. 'Let's go.'

Instinct overrode the calm, controlled, adult way in which she'd hoped to handle this. Defensively, she hitched her tote up onto her shoulder.

'It's not the fifties, Leon. I think we can agree you've already done enough to "help", thank you very much.'

When she saw her words lance through his eyes, she regretted her sharp tone. She was floundering as much as he must be. She'd walloped him with a reality he had never wanted. She might not want to marry the man because… *bleurgh, feelings*…but she respected him professionally at least. And you didn't treat people you respected as if they were the enemy.

She tried again. 'Honestly, Leon. I'm fine. We can meet later, if you like, but I'm okay to find the hotel on my own.'

'Lizzy—' He caught hold of her hand, preventing her from leaving.

She tugged it free. *What the hell?* Her father had never hit her mother, but this was one of his standard moves. Holding her in place until he felt he'd been *heard.* She took back the respect thing. Respect had to be earned, and this sort of behaviour was not the way to start cashing in.

'Back off—all right?'

He held up his hands, but the energy emanating from him kept her caught in its snare.

'You have just told me you're pregnant with my child. *Our* child.'

He swept his fingers through his hair, and her body lived the sensation as if she'd done it herself.

'You've had time to digest this. Don't you think I deserve some time, too?' He took a steadying breath, then continued. 'My response might be clumsier than you'd like, but pushing me away isn't going to help either of us. Or the child.'

It was a fair point. Not that it stopped her heart from hammering against her ribcage or muted the fight-or-flight response her body was incapable of shaking off.

She forced herself to look at him—really look at this man who'd just been told he was going to father a child—and tried to see things from his perspective. What she saw made her heart stop and then do precisely what she'd willed it not to. Crack open far enough to allow the compassion she'd hoped to keep at bay pour in.

He looked every bit as scared and braced for battle and—yes—as strangely hopeful as *she'd* felt when she'd first taken the test.

Which, of course, added a ream of complications to what she'd hoped would be a black and white situation. She would tell him. He would say *Best of luck, mate*—or whatever the Italian equivalent of 'mate' was. Certainly not *pata-tina*, as he'd used to jokingly call her: his little potato. And then off she'd pop, back to Australia, to get on with the rest of her life, raising a child who would, one day, inevitably want to meet the man its mother had made love to as if her life depended upon it.

That was how intense it had been. Her need to get him in and out of her system during that one unexpected night.

As far as plans backfiring went, this was shaping up to be a doozy.

She forced herself to meet his gaze directly. 'Let's get a move on, shall we?'

CHAPTER FOUR

SIDE BY SIDE, Leon guided Lizzy through the busy hospital corridors, hoping she couldn't see his frown periodically quirking into a smile.

Same old Lizzy. Fiery. Fierce. As combative as ever when it came to good old-fashioned chivalry. As if an offer to open a door would lead to a life of indentured servitude.

The last thing in the world Leon wanted to do was trap Lizzy in 'a patriarchal system designed to subvert women for the sole purpose of big-upping male egos.' Her words. Not his. Something, he suspected, to do with her father—a leading cardiologist who, suffice it to say, wasn't known for his bedside manner.

They'd never really talked about their pasts, but he presumed if her relationship with her father had been warm, she definitely would have pulled him and his experience into conversation much more frequently than never.

He'd messed up big-time by grabbing her

wrist, but he'd meant it when he'd said he would look after her. Her surprise announcement had tapped into the instinctive part of him that didn't just *want* to be protective—it *had* to be.

A child.

He, Leon Cassanetti—sworn bachelor and slave to his professional calling, a man who brought new life into the world for other people—already knew in his heart that he was going to cross that thick line he'd drawn in the sand between himself and the rest of the world. So much for the years he'd spent ensuring he was the kind of clear-eyed physician who kept his perspective purely scientific.

Emotions were things his patients dealt with. Men and women who, for reasons he'd thought he'd never understand, had decided to risk the foundations of their emotional stability by bringing a child into the world.

His arrival had signalled the beginning of the end for his own parents. What was it signalling for him and Lizzy?

To stop his thoughts reeling too far out of control, he forced himself to focus on the immediate pragmatics of their situation. He rang ahead to Reception, where she'd stored her luggage, to have it follow them in a taxi, and cleared his calendar for the rest of the day, all the while try-ing to push his mother's well-worn edict out of his mind: *Keep everyone at arm's length and all will be well.*

He glanced down at Lizzy as they made their way silently to the underground car park where he kept his scooter. There were light shadows under her eyes. She had just flown halfway around the world, but now that he looked at her—really looked—he saw that tell-tale glow about her. The one that assured him, without needing scientific proof, that she was carry-ing a child. There was an added lustre to her harvest-coloured hair, an extra wattage in the flares of connection they shared each time their eyes met.

He stopped abruptly, the memory of a col-league's experience bringing an unwelcome rush of adrenaline. 'I can't drive you there.'

She looked up at him, confused. The crinkle he'd used to run his thumb along to smooth away her worries formed between her brows. He shook off the instinct to do the same again.

'I brought my scooter,' he explained.

She shrugged in a way that suggested he was being ridiculous. 'Do you have an extra helmet?'

He did. And they had spares at the hospital's concierge desk. But—no.

'A car would be safer.'

'I'm not made of delicate crystal, Leon.'

'You are carrying our child.'

She crossed her arms and fixed him with a humourless smile. 'Interesting. Is this what you tell all your patients? That they should ride in crash-proof vehicles, wrapped in cotton wool, until they've delivered?'

She fixed him with a look suggesting that he had lost some brain cells between here and the antenatal unit. There was very possibly some truth to that. He was wading into something so unfamiliar to him he had no idea if he'd sink or swim.

She continued in her usual brisk, almost casually amused way. 'You know as well as I do that women have been getting on with their lives whilst pregnant for thousands of years. I'm guessing countless pregnant women right here in Rome have ridden scooters to and from their hotels with—'

She stopped herself, her upper teeth snagging her lower lip. Second thoughts, maybe? Or, more likely, feeling the enormity of what was happening now that they were together, absorbing the reality that in six months they would be having a child together.

As if on cue a young couple walked by, the woman carrying a newborn, cooing and whispering loving phrases of nonsense, the euphoria of having brought a life into the world blurring everything else.

Lizzy's eyes followed them, then clouded with a rush of emotion he couldn't put his finger on.

'Are you all right, *cara*?'

She didn't meet his eyes. 'Fine. C'mon. Let's go.'

They finished the walk to his scooter in silence.

Was this how the next few months would be? Each shared activity a small tug of war? One of them gaining a handhold here, the other the next, until at last their hands touched in the centre or, more likely, one fell down?

When he handed her his spare helmet, their fingers brushing as they made the exchange, he saw the tiniest hint of fragility fissure through the facade of the strongest woman he'd ever met. She caught him looking and once again looked away.

He frowned. This wasn't how he wanted things to go. He didn't want her to take his every suggestion as a power-play. He respected her. He cared for her. He might not have imagined a proper relationship or having a family with her, but that wasn't their reality any more. They'd have to figure it out. Together.

After he'd secured her helmet and climbed on, signalling Lizzy to climb on behind him, a suspicion rose. He knew exactly why she'd abruptly balked at the thought of a scooter ride. She was going to have to put her arms around him. Rest her hands on his hips at the very least.

When she climbed onto the seat behind him he felt the thrill of connection for a nanosecond. Then she pulled back, trying to keep a few centimetres of space between them. He revved the scooter and took off. Her hands instantly swooped round his waist.

He did his best not to respond to her touch… not to lean into those hot licks of response as her breasts brushed along his back. But it proved impossible as, with turn after turn, her fingers wove more tightly around his waist as if they'd done this a thousand times. To the point where he allowed himself a careless thought… *What if this was their reality?* Riding to and from work together…her hands round his waist…her breasts pressing into his back.

His hand instinctively slipped to her leg at some traffic lights, giving her thigh a light rub that spoke to all the feelings he felt for her but wasn't equipped to put a voice to. He hadn't been given the classic Italian gift for florid speech. The ability so many men had to call a woman *amore* or *cara*. Loved one. Dearest. Those words meant something pure and deep-seeded. Words that should only be spoken if the speaker had the emotional foundation to back them up. It was why he'd never called a woman *amore*, not even when he'd met Lizzy, opting instead for the more comical *patatina*.

'This doesn't look like a hotel.' Lizzy pointed up to the stone-and-marble-faced building he'd stopped in front of.

'No. It's my apartment building.'

Lizzy gave him the kind of double take he would've given himself if he'd been looking in a mirror. He was fiercely protective of his own space. Even in New York, where prices were insane and sharing a flat would've made so much sense—particularly for two people who spent the bulk of their spare time together—they'd each kept their own small studios, using the on-call rooms at the hospital more often than either of those.

He allowed himself a snapshot memory of their naked bodies tangled together, bedclothes heaven knew where, wishing fervently that dawn would never come.

'I thought I was staying at a hotel.' Her voice was guarded.

'This makes more sense.'

'To whom, exactly?'

'The both of us. *Per favore*. I have a guest room, so you'll have your own space. If it's too strange I'll take you to the hotel, but we have a lot to discuss.'

'That doesn't mean I have to stay with you to discuss it.'

No. But it did mean more hoops to jump through, and one thing neither of them had was excess time.

'Lizzy. Please. I want you to stay with me.'

For ever?

He didn't miss the sceptical narrowing of her eyes as, wordlessly, she climbed off the scooter.

'This isn't the largest of lifts, is it?' she crabbed as the two of them got into the small, wrought-iron-gated elevator built some seventy-odd years back. It moved so slowly he sometimes wondered if it was run by mice on a treadmill.

He looked down at the space between them, suddenly vividly aware that in six months' time it wouldn't be empty. It would be filled with the round, beautifully weighted orb of Lizzy's belly. Her hands might be resting on it to feel a kick or a squirm. Or his hands...

He stopped the daydream when his fingers twitched at the urge to massage oil into her back and belly to ease the strain her pregnancy might be taking on her. To hold their baby in his arms the moment it was born, then carry it to her so she, too, could embrace the tiny, beautiful child they'd created.

An unwelcome alternative arose. In six months' time Lizzy might be back in Sydney.

'How's your mother?' Lizzy asked, clearly uncomfortable in the silence. 'Is she still in Rome?'

'I'm afraid she passed away recently.'

All the fractiousness crackling between them disappeared. 'Oh, Leon. I'm so sorry. I didn't know or I would've—'

He waved away her apologies. 'Honestly. It's fine.'

It wasn't. It had knocked him for six. But in ways he hadn't expected. Ways that had given him mad ideas like inviting Lizzy Beckley to Rome. Into his *home*.

It was surprising to realise that what pained him was wondering what would've happened if he hadn't rung Lizzy. Would she have told him she was pregnant? The thought stuck like the poisoned tip of a blackthorn in his conscience. Of all the things he'd allowed Lizzy to know about him on a personal front, two things rose to the fore: he didn't want children and he didn't want a relationship.

Two long-held beliefs that had done a complete one-eighty in the space of an hour. Heaven knew what the next hour had in store—let alone the next six months.

'I always thought you became a maternal foetal medicine specialist because of her,' Lizzy said softly.

It was a leading question and they both knew it. Leon had never spoken about his mother to Lizzy. Talking about her was opening a can of worms and looking into a past that he would happily keep closed for ever.

He shook his head, but wondered if perhaps there was some truth to it. If a mother wasn't well, the child or children she was carrying would suffer. His mother has suffered enormous mental anguish. Relationship PTSD. The trauma and hurt had gone that deep. As such, Leon had not been immune either.

'Was she still living here in Rome?' Lizzy asked.

He gave a soft smile, grateful for the topic-change. 'Yes. I don't think anything could have pulled her away from here.'

'No?'

He shook his head and smiled. His mother might not have won any parenting prizes, but she had been a character. A very colour-ful character. And, more to the point, she had taught him not so much the power of love, but the fierceness of loyalty. When his father had left them, she'd stayed. Fed him, clothed him, drilled questionable survival skills into him when a piece of him had always known, but rarely acknowledged, that his mother would have liked to do exactly what his father had... walked away when the going got tough and pre-tended he didn't exist.

He cleared his throat and answered neutrally. 'She was a dedicated Roman. Occasionally, when the tourist population grew too much in the summertime, she could be tempted out to the Mediterranean... If the boyfriend was right.'

'She never remarried, then?'

'No,' he laughed. 'Pigs would've flown before my mother agreed to marry again.'

Lizzy's lips tweaked into a smile, but he could see her connecting these dots she'd not had access to before.

They'd had a very clear 'Don't Ask, Don't Tell' rule back in the day. His past was messy, emotional and unsettling. He knew very little of Lizzy's, but she had seemed equally happy not to air her childhood laundry. It was an unspoken policy that had worked for them right up until an hour ago. Now that they were going to have a child everything would have to change. And that included the way he looked at his own life.

Leon had never questioned his mother's embittered approach to love because he'd borne witness to its source. His father had never given her a reason for his abrupt departure. He'd simply risen from the supper table one night and walked away. Boarded a plane. Sent word through a secretary that he'd send a courier for his things and that had pretty much been that. No explanation. No hugs goodbye.

The experience had thrown Leon into the heart of the savage pain of loss. A loss so profound he refused to open himself up to that level of hurt and rejection again. Which had landed him here, in the world's slowest lift, with the woman who was carrying his child and, by all accounts, didn't want him involved in his child's life. A woman, in short, who didn't trust him as far as she could throw him.

He glanced again at Lizzy's flat belly and the space between them. Pictured the child that would one day come into the world and tried to imagine sitting down with him or her and teaching all the distrust and wariness his own mother had taught him.

What a selfish thing to do. An even more selfish way to love. The anguish his mother must have felt, to teach her child that his love would never be returned, must have been devastating.

He saw in a flash that what his mother had done was no better than his father's abrupt departure. He'd always thought he'd been protecting Lizzy and himself from an inevitable pain. But what he'd actually done was smash the foundations of what might have been an amazing relationship. If she'd wanted one.

Now that she was going to have his child would she want one? The chemistry was obviously still there. The professional respect. But the love...?

A tang of well-trained panic rose in his throat.

Lizzy looked up, a question in her eyes. 'Are you all right, Leon?'

'Marry me.'

She actually barked with laughter. 'Don't be mad.'

'I mean it, Lizzy.'

To his shock, he did. Mostly. Yes. Definitely. They could be a family. Here in Rome. At her place in Sydney. Wherever. He had no idea how it would work, but he did know he didn't want his son or daughter feeling the blunt heartache of rejection the way he had.

'Marry you?' Lizzy said dryly, and gave him an intense look as if scanning him for signs of insanity.

'I'm not the worst option.'

This elicited a trill of laughter too quickly. 'Nor are you the best.'

Her words pierced a place in his heart he hadn't even known existed. 'There's someone else?'

Indignation flared in her eyes, then reformed as a blaze of strength. 'I don't think my personal life is any of your business. Apart, of course, from the baby.'

Her hand instinctively went to her belly just

as the lift churned the final few inches towards the top-floor flat.

'I'll be a father to this child,' he said, placing his hand over hers. 'Our child. And a husband to you. It's the right thing to do. It's my duty.'

CHAPTER FIVE

'No!' Lizzy laughed as she spoke, but her heart was slamming against her ribcage so hard it physically hurt.

Marry him? It was the one question she had privately ached to hear five years before—but this way? Being brought to his flat without being asked. Being told he would parent their child without even considering the plans she'd already made for the baby? And she had plans, all right. Lots of plans. In Australia. Without him.

And marriage as a *duty*?

No. Freaking. Way.

It was exactly what her parents had done. Her mother had fallen pregnant during her first year out of uni. After a long talk between their fathers, Lizzy's parents had 'enjoyed' a shotgun wedding. And her father had never let her mother forget it. He stayed out of duty. Nothing more.

'No, what?' Leon persisted, as if there was any other question blinking in huge neon letters between them.

'No, I will not marry you,' she said more solidly. 'Not under these circumstances.'

Because he didn't really mean it. Right?

'Why not?' Leon asked, in the same way he might ask her why she thought a tricky surgery couldn't or, more to the point, shouldn't be performed.

It's not possible, came the small voice in her head.

A flare of light flashed through his eyes. She knew what it was. The acceptance of a challenge.

'Anything's possible, Lizzy.'

He'd used to say that all the time, back when they'd shared an operating theatre.

'You just have to find the right path.'

Lizzy ignored the tiniest waver fluttering through her heart and fixed him with her best *Be serious* look. Shutting him down was easier than pouring her heart out to him. Telling him she'd watched her mother fade from a beautiful, happy, smiling woman into a timorous, fearful shadow of a mouse, back-seating her own fledgling career as a social worker to support her husband and daughter.

How could Lizzy admit to someone so strong and solid that there was a part of her terrified of discovering that he would be like her father? A man who ruled with a *Because I said so* edict. And that, to keep the peace, she'd follow it. There was no way she could give up on everything she'd worked so hard for to enter into a marriage of emotional oppression and control.

When her mother had died three years back, never having received the love she'd so desperately deserved, something had changed in Lizzy. Hardened. She had vowed, then and there, never to let herself fall into the same trap. Never to live in a marriage hoping and praying for the day when her husband would finally realise he'd loved her all along.

Leon didn't budge, his expression expectant. *'You just have to find the right path.'*

Seriously? Did he genuinely want her to consider this as an actual proposal?

Married. A family. With Leon.

It was exactly what Lizzy had dreamt of all their years apart, so why did it feel more like a nightmare than a dream come true?

Because he had asked out of duty. Out of a need to control the situation. Not out of love.

Something must have changed in her expression, because after a moment of stillness his hand left hers and his eyes locked on the arrow inching its way to the seventh floor. From the brusque way he yanked open the lift door and crossed the marble-floored corridor to his flat, she wasn't holding out much hope that a declaration of undying love was forthcoming.

Missing Leon's touch upon her belly more than she cared to admit, she dazedly followed him into what was a surprisingly soulless apartment. A feat, considering how incredible it was. Floor-to-ceiling windows. Bifold doors that would open wide to the fresh spring afternoon. Richly coloured rugs took the echoey edge off the marble floors. Immaculate sofas formed an arc around a modern fireplace. Tactical displays of tulips dotted about the rest of the relatively monochrome furnishings provided bright, primary splashes of colour. Black and white photographs that might have been taken by anyone, anywhere, lined the walls.

It was more show home than comfort zone, unlike her own tiny house back in Sydney. It was her beachside cocoon away from the hospital where, every now and again, she had to rebuild herself after particularly tough cases. Her refrigerator was covered in crayon drawings. Her windowsills were filled with thank-you cards for her and her lodger, Byron, a scrub nurse who also worked at the children's hospital.

There were no signs of Leon's professional calling here. She had an entire wall made up of photos of proud parents holding the babies she'd helped bring into the world. The joy they elicited in her was as powerful as if they were family members. This place looked as if it had hardly been lived in—if at all. The building itself had an old-fashioned exterior that spoke of a deep human presence, but up here on the seventh floor...

She couldn't put her finger on it, exactly, but it felt lonely up here. Which, unexpectedly, made her heart ache for Leon.

The one place she warmed to as Leon gave her a swift tour of the two guest rooms she could choose between and the open-plan kitchen with its pristine marble breakfast bar, was the terrace that wrapped all the way around the building. It was wider than a balcony and canvas awnings were dotted about it, creating little protected seating areas, and just outside the kitchen there was a breakfast area where Leon said you could watch the sun rise.

'And…do you do that?' she asked, conscious that both of them were avoiding the 'Marry me' elephant in the room. 'Watch the sunrise?'

He shrugged. 'If I'm here and I see it, yes. If not, no.'

The response seemed so bereft of any engagement in his actual life that she had to ask. 'What do you do for fun?'

He looked at her, confused. 'Fun?'

'Yeah…' She warmed to the topic. 'You know—that thing we used to have back in the day, when we weren't in surgery?'

A midnight picnic they'd once shared in a sloshy bubble bath sprang to mind. Leon, however, still looked confused.

'I thought the *surgeries* were fun. The stuff in between was—'

He stopped himself, his eyes meeting hers, and she knew as they did that he'd been caught out. The 'stuff in between' had always been the two of them. Giggling over lattes and warm blueberry muffins as they rehashed the day's surgical rotation. Bashing out their frustrations if there'd been a run-in with a superior at a nearby batting cage, both of them ending up in hysterics over how bad they were as neither of them had grown up playing baseball. And, of course, the countless hours they'd spent in bed, not just making love but daydreaming of a time and a place when performing surgery would be second nature to them and the rest of their energies could be poured into enjoying life the way the rest of their peers who were already established surgeons did.

When she looked at it that way—clinically—she couldn't believe she hadn't seen it before. All their interactions in New York had been work-related. Well. Work and sex-related. What a fool to think he might have loved her as she'd loved him.

Channelling the woman who seemed capable of asking all the questions she'd kept to herself for the last five years, she plopped her tote onto one of the breakfast bar stools and challenged him. 'Go on. You were saying…?' She held her hands out. 'The stuff in between surgeries was what, exactly? A time-filler? Meaningless? Fond memories?'

The last words came out a bit more angrily than it should have if she actually wanted to know the answer.

He gave the back of his neck a scrub. 'It was

great, Lizzy. You know that. It was time with you.' He pulled his hand up through his hair and rubbed his eyes. 'Look. You're tired, and I'm still digesting. I think it'd be a good idea if you had a rest. I'll go out and get us some food.'

She felt riled again. Would he *stop* telling her what to do?

He pulled open the refrigerator door and showed her the sparse pickings, as if to prove he wasn't making up an excuse to leave her on her own. A tiny bit of her fury drifted away. Okay. Fine. So maybe he was telling the truth about that part.

'When you get up, we'll eat and talk about this properly—*all* of this. Tomorrow's going to be the first time the full team meets to discuss the twins' treatment, so I'm as aware as you are that we need to find some sort of happy place, *si*?'

Ha! Happy place? The man was mad.

She wanted to protest. Insist that now was the right time to talk. Sending her off to her room like a naughty child was just the sort of thing her father would have done if she'd dared to question his judgement. Saying that…there had been compassion in Leon's voice. Concern.

Enough to throw her off her guard and, more pressingly, allow room for the jet-leg that adrenaline had been holding at bay to flood in.

She'd done the hardest part. She'd told him she was having their child. And rather than run away, which had been pretty much her number one choice of options for him, he'd stayed. Proposed, even. Offered her everything she'd ever wanted from him in the space of a lift journey. Everything apart from his undying love.

If there had been an eighth floor, would that declaration have revealed itself?

She considered insisting they talk it out now, but knew the chances that things would quickly degenerate because of her increasing fatigue were high. He was right. Annoyingly.

A huge yawn threatened to consume the remains of her brain cells, all but proving his point that she needed some rest. Reluctantly she acquiesced, and all but tumbled into one of the guest rooms, where a large wooden sleigh bed with a gorgeously inviting duvet beckoned her into a sound, dreamless slumber.

Several hours later she woke feelingly surprisingly refreshed. There were sounds of cutlery and plates clattering in the kitchen. Her phone, which had adjusted itself to the local time, said it was just gone seven p.m.

She walked barefoot into the kitchen in the airline T-shirt she'd managed to tug on before falling asleep. It was a hand-me-down from Byron, whose long-term boyfriend was a pilot.

Leon had also changed. In place of the navy scrubs he wore twill trousers which made the most of his long legs, and a white linen shirt that hung from his shoulders as if it were made to measure. His dark eyes met hers as she walked into the room, brightening in the first instance and then, as he took in her ensemble, emptying of light.

She tugged on the hem and threw him an apology. 'Sorry. I should've showered and dressed before coming out. I just heard you in here and wanted to make sure I had time before…you know…proceedings get underway.'

He didn't laugh at the sonorous voice she'd put on, instead giving one of those indeterminate head-shakes—*yes, no, whatever you wish.* He was being weird.

She looked down at the T-shirt. It was very clearly a man's. Did he think—?

'Like it? It's my housemate's. It's comfy to

sleep in. Not exactly as stylish as I know you Italians are, but it does the trick.'

'You live with a man?'

Leon feigned an air of casual indifference to the point where it was actually kind of adorable. Leon Cassanetti... Jealous of a man he had no need to be jealous of. How long should she let this play out before she told him Byron was her very gay housemate, who would never in a million years like women?

Leon tipped some antipasti into a bowl and pretty much missed the bowl. Definitely not a precision surgical move. Maybe she'd let this play out just a little bit.

She smiled, nabbing one of the amazing olives. Why was food so much better in Italy?

Leon bashed a glass against the tap, realised he'd cracked it, then threw it in the bin with a low curse.

Okay. Maybe she should explain...

'A few years back, when I bought my place, I thought it'd be wise to reduce the mortgage payments by having a housemate. Byron—one of the scrub nurses at the hospital—heard me talking about whether or not to let the room and volunteered himself. I thought... Why not?'

'Oh. Right...' Leon swept up a newly spilt

pool of olive oil from the counter. 'So you two are colleagues, are you?'

'And friends.'

He began to chop some carrots with a pronounced *thunk* of the knife after each incision.

This was fun. And a little bit mean.

Her commitment to making Leon sweat was already wavering—which didn't really speak well to the whole getting custody of their child sorted, moving back to Australia and not worrying about seeing him ever again thing. Or maybe the fact that he'd proposed had given short shrift to that.

'So…you two socialise?' Leon asked.

'Byron is the only reason I *have* a social life,' she answered truthfully.

After her tenure in New York, and landing her job at Sydney's premier children's hospital, she'd fallen into a pattern that had been eighty percent hospital, fifteen percent sleep and the other five pretty much devoted to eating in front of the telly. Byron wouldn't have any of it, saying that life was for living, not box-setting. He'd said she was too pretty and too young to hang up her stilettos just yet. He'd even been the one to set up her profile on a rarely used dating app.

When she could see Leon trying and failing to find another question to ascertain if she and Byron were 'friends with benefits' she finally broke. She hadn't come here to be cruel. 'We occasionally go to the movies or a concert when he's not out with his boyfriend. Which is a lot.'

Leon's shoulders lowered about three inches, and his smile finally allowed a hint of the playfulness she'd once had full access to to surface.

'Could you maybe consider putting some more clothes on?' he asked.

His eyes dropped to her thighs and swept back up her body with such specificity that she felt her nipples grow taut against the soft cotton of the loose top. That was when it hit her. Leon still found her attractive. She didn't know why she had discounted that as an option. She gulped. He might have actually meant it when he'd asked her to marry him.

Heat sprang to her cheeks and, unable to sustain the eye contact he'd locked her in, she shot out of the room, took a quick, very cold shower, put on her most shapeless clothes and marched back into the kitchen, ready to deliver the little speech she'd rehearsed on the plane.

'I didn't come here to corner you into marrying me.'

Leon handed her a plate of antipasti, his lips parting in protest.

She held up a hand. 'Please. I'd like to get through this—mostly because I've been practising it for so long. I just need to get it out, okay?'

He nodded, poured her a glass of fizzy water, then joined her at the breakfast bar, giving her his full, undivided attention. Something her father definitely wouldn't have done.

'Okay. So… As you have probably guessed, my being pregnant is as much of a surprise to me as it is to you—but, as you say, I've had more time to digest. And, having given it a lot of thought, I definitely want to keep the baby.'

He nodded, his eyebrows burrowing together as if not keeping it hadn't even factored on his radar. It was another arrow into her heart. The warm, fuzzy kind that made saying the next part more difficult.

'My plan is to live in Australia. There will be no financial burden on you. Or emotional. Or anything else that you don't want. However, when the baby—my child—is old enough, I want to secure your permission for him or her to reach out to you… You know… To meet their biological father.'

'No.'

Lizzy physically recoiled at the bluntness of his response. 'What do you mean, no?'

CHAPTER SIX

LEON ALMOST REGRETTED not pouring himself a glass of wine, but he knew keeping a clear head was critical.

He took Lizzy's hand in his, trying not to react when she pulled it away, balled it into a fist and tucked it onto her lap under the counter. This wasn't just her child they were talking about. It was *theirs*. Their child. Their future. And that meant everything he'd believed before was now rendered null and void.

Did he know if he was capable of being a good husband? No. Would he be a good father? Perhaps better than his own, but that wasn't saying a lot. It would be a learning curve. A sharp one. But he'd never shied away from anything that scared him. Apart, of course, from relationships.

He started again. 'I meant our child won't have to seek me out because it is going to be a part of my life—*our* lives—from day one, so there will be no need for him or her to reach out, because I will already have been there every step of the way.'

His insides were echoing Lizzy's expression. One that very clearly asked, *Who stole the real Leon and replaced him with you?*

But rather than smile and relax with relief at the prospect of shared parenthood, her frown deepened.

It stung him to know that the deepest impression he'd made on her was one of non-interest. It stung more to realise she hadn't been kidding when she'd said she didn't want him to be part of their child's life.

'Leon…' She teased at a loose string on her cuff. 'I live in Australia.'

He waved his hand between them. 'Logistics. You could live here. I could move there. We commute. Whatever it takes.'

'Bullshit.'

'Che cosa?'

'I said bullshit. You don't want to be married and have a family. I mean—' She gestured towards his flat. 'Look at this place. This isn't the type of home you'd buy if you wanted little ones and a wife around, is it?'

He took a look at the flat through her eyes.

Chrome. Glass. Clean, clear lines. Nothing out of place except the jumper Lizzy had thrown on the back of a chair—which, he had to admit, he'd been itching to fold into an exact square and put back in her room.

La merda. She was right. Not a solitary thing in this flat spoke to a latent craving to be part of a family. And yet with Lizzy here, the place already felt nicer to come home to.

He gave himself a psychological thump on the back. She was right. He liked things as they were. But a child… A child changed everything.

'I could move. We could find somewhere together.'

'Oh!' She laughed. 'Sure! You could absolutely move. But not with me.' She said it with a smile, but her voice was fuelled by fierce protectiveness. 'I repeat: you don't want to be a father, Leon. You don't want to be married.'

'Nor do you,' he countered. 'At least you didn't back in New York.'

'I don't exactly remember you asking!' she snapped in a way that betrayed a vulnerability he'd never seen before.

Oh, hell. She'd wanted him to ask.

But they'd both talked so often about pursuing their careers—hers in Sydney, his in Rome—

he'd just presumed it really was what they'd both wanted.

She flicked her hair over her shoulders and continued the speech she'd clearly rehearsed. 'You'd have to change your approach to work. And home-life, such as it is. There will be toys everywhere. And laundry. You'll be woken up in the middle of the night by the crying of a baby that you don't get paid to look after. And let's be honest, Leon. The only thing you want to be woken up by in the middle of the night is your beeper.'

'Lizzy,' he began, using his *now, let's be sensible* voice, 'if you can change, what makes you think I can't?'

She gave one solitary bark of laughter and shook her head in a vague way, her eyes not leaving his, as if answering the question would give him an opportunity to pounce and take control.

'I've *met* you, Leon.' Her features softened. 'Look. I'm not trying to be cruel. Honestly. I'm trying to be realistic. So…can we just take this whole "marry me" thing off the table?'

He scrubbed his hand over his face. He wanted to do the best by her. And now that he'd seen that glimpse of a part of her he'd never seen before—the part that had hoped for a long-term relationship...

No. She was right. He wasn't equipped for love, marriage or a baby carriage. How could he be? He'd been trained from an early age to think that love brought pain. Parenting equalled abandonment. But if Lizzy, a woman who had been very clear about not wanting children herself, could climb aboard the bandwagon, why couldn't he?

Because she didn't want him to be a part of it.

She was walking away years before his father had. Which, in some ways, was kinder than his father had been. But in other ways...?

His chest flooded with emotion, clouding his judgement as he tried to figure out the best way to proceed.

Lizzy, eagle-eyed, saw his indecision and slapped her hand on the marble countertop in frustration. 'We're not discussing real estate here, Leon. Or career moves. Or beepers. We're discussing a child. A baby. One I hadn't planned on having and one I know for sure you hadn't. Marrying you isn't going to put a nice pretty bow on everything and make it better.' She swept her hands along her cheeks and gave the back of her neck a rub. 'Look...

How about this? Tomorrow, let's put our focus where it should be. On the twins. Then, after a few days, when we're both thinking a bit more clearly, let's do a scan together.'

'Have you seen it? The baby?'

She threw him a look as if he'd lost his marbles. 'I'm thirteen weeks pregnant, Leon.'

Yes. She'd seen it.

'Seen it and heard the heartbeat,' she confirmed.

His breath left his chest with such force it was as if he'd been kicked. In its place a memory shot to the fore.

A couple completely in love with each other who had been unable to physically be with their child during the Covid outbreak when it had developed pneumonia. He'd told himself at the time that heartache like theirs was exactly why he didn't want to be in a relationship. Now he saw how wrong he'd been. If he messed things up with Lizzy, he'd be the one on the outside looking in and he didn't like it. Not one damn bit.

He refilled Lizzy's water glass and took a sip of his own before speaking. 'I don't know how things were for you in Sydney during the Covid outbreak, but at St Nicolino's we had people standing outside the hospital, hoping and praying their children would know they were there. Making video calls if they could…showing their child how close they were. One carer per family was eventually allowed in the hospital, but even then they often weren't allowed in the room. Siblings weren't allowed in at all. For far too many families the more relaxed visiting rules came too late. It was absolutely heartbreaking. As if the loss of a child wasn't enough, they weren't able to comfort one another as the situation worsened.'

'Yes…' she nodded, clearly having had a similar experience '…and your point is?'

'My mum. Her death.' He held up a hand to stop any flow of sympathies. He wasn't digging. He was explaining. 'When she died…the truth was, it was hard for me to feel anything.'

She furrowed her brow, clearly confused. 'What do you mean?'

He shook his head, still trying to figure it out himself. 'It was like my mother had created her own lockdown bubble around herself twenty-five years ago when my father left. I hadn't realised just how much she'd restricted access to herself until after she passed, when there was very little change in my life. In anyone's, really.'

Shockingly little. And although he'd only admitted it to himself as he'd shouldered the weight of her coffin along with five strangers he'd realised he'd barely known her. No wonder he approached life so scientifically. So clinically. It was the only emotional toolbox he'd been given access to.

Lizzy slid her arms into a tight cross over her chest. 'I thought you liked to keep yourself apart from all that messy emotional stuff.'

'I do. Emotional distance as a surgeon is essential. You know that. Emotion clouds judgement.'

She harrumphed.

'I believe that. *Professionally*,' he clarified. 'But as a son I was never given the chance to be emotional about my family.'

Not in public anyway. He'd felt the pain of abandonment when his father had left. The gradual cooling of affections as his mother had withdrawn her own.

He tapped his finger on the countertop, then looked up to meet Lizzy's eyes. 'It took my mother dying in the way she did—isolated, friendless—for me to realise that no matter how much you convince yourself keeping people you care about at a distance will help, it doesn't. It just means you'll be alone when you die.'

'And that's your big revelation from all this? You don't want to be alone when you die?' Lizzy couldn't keep the scepticism from her voice.

'No.' He shook his head, then looked her square in the eye. 'I don't want to be alone when I live.'

He watched his words land and take hold of her the same way the news he was going to be a father had gripped his heart and pressed the air out of his lungs in one swift blow.

She squeezed her eyes tight, then opened them, the aquamarine clarity of them piercing through to his chest. Somewhere deep within that kaleidoscope of blues and greens a *yes* was floating about, waiting to find purchase. A *yes* to the question he'd never imagined himself asking. *Will you marry me*?

Everything in him stilled as he waited for her to speak. If she said yes, he was going to have to throw himself at the relationship learning curve with the same blind focus he'd used when he'd poured himself into his career.

Lizzy shifted in her chair and ran her finger round the rim of her glass. 'Maybe we should hold off deciding exactly what we're going to do. Like you said, I have jet lag and you have…' she scrubbed the air between them '…your "issues".'

It wasn't a no. It wasn't a *yes, let's all move in and play happy families* either, but they had time to figure out what to do without… *Ha!* Without letting all this emotion cloud their judgement. *As if.*

Just as he was about to suggest they move to the table out on the terrace and eat some of the antipasti he'd bought at the local *salumeria*, his mobile rang.

'Pronto?'

He locked eyes with Lizzy as he took in the details of the call. This was much more familiar terrain. An infant needing immediate surgery. The prematurely born boy had struggled with necrotising enterocolitis and the situation, which had been steadily monitored throughout his stay in the NICU, had reached critical. It was one of the most common problems for premature infants, but its likelihood made it no less lethal.

He rattled off a few instructions, ending the call with a promise to be there and gowned up within fifteen minutes.

'NEC?' Lizzy asked when he'd ended the call.

He nodded, then did a double-take. 'Your Italian's a lot better than you let on back at the hospital.'

She shrugged, as if it was completely natural that she should have added Italian to her list of skills over the years. 'I know enough to get by.'

No. She knew enough to move to Italy if she'd ever been asked.

He pocketed the information for later, pulled his jacket off the back of the chair he'd hung it on, scooped his keys from the ceramic bowl where he always deposited them at the end of a long day, when he propped himself up on one of the stools to eat yet another takeaway meal before crawling into bed and, a few hours later, waking up to start another day.

He looked up when Lizzy pointedly cleared her throat. Rather than looking annoyed that he was leaving, she looked expectant. As if awaiting an invitation. An invitation he knew she would accept.

'Want to come?' he asked. 'You don't have to. You can stay and sleep, eat—'

'No. I'd like to come.' She ran to her room and came back out tugging a sweater over her shoulders. 'Are we running or jumping on the scooter?'

'Scooter.'

Waiting for the lift seemed a waste of time, so by silent agreement they began to jog down the stairs, with Leon filling her in as they went.

'Luca Ricci was born fifteen weeks premature. He's been poorly for the duration of his stay in the NICU—infections in his bloodstream, problems with breathing—but lately he's been exhibiting intolerance to milk feeds. We've been trying to keep the intestinal inflammation to a minimum by introducing intravenous feeds, antibiotics and an abdominal drain, but it looks as though some of the bowel has become so damaged it's begun to necrotise.'

'What signs is he showing just now?'

'Swollen stomach. Dark external colouration indicating a further perforation. Bradycardia.'

Lizzy doubled her speed on the stairs. 'I've had a few of those back in Sydney.' She scrunched up her face. 'Do the parents know the risks?'

'Fifty-fifty chance of survival?' Leon put the cold hard truth into words. 'Yes. They know. But it's that fifty percent of children who make it that we're focused on, *si*?'

'*Si, Dottore*.' Lizzy gave him a small salute before accepting the helmet he was handing her.

None of the awkwardness of their first ride

returned as, focused on the surgery ahead, the two of them climbed onto the scooter. Lizzy's hands slipped around his waist as if they'd done it for years and off they went.

Half an hour later the pair of them were in scrubs, standing on either side of an operating table with the small infant between them, all the earlier hostilities and tensions that had been vibrating between the pair of them evaporated.

It was just as it had been back in their surgical internships. Two focused, perfectionist surgeons working together with a harmony he'd let himself forget they shared. The Dream Team, the residents had called them. The Down Under Wonder and Da Vinci.

She'd come up with that one, Da Vinci, because he'd look at the same 'canvas' they all did and, where many of their peers only saw dead ends, see nothing but possibility.

'You just have to find the right path.' *H*is mantra.

He looked across at her and she gave him an *Are you ready?* nod, hands up, ready for action. It was a silent signal to let him know that wherever he would go, she would follow.

For the first time the gesture spoke volumes.

She trusted him. Here at least. In the operating theatre.

Had there been a time when Lizzy had seen a completely different path? One that had included their careers and the two of them together. *Dio mio.* That must have been why she'd learned Italian. Because she'd believed that one day he would call. Admit he'd been wrong not to admit that he'd heard her whisper that she loved him and tell her that he felt the same way.

He threw the thought away, needing to focus on the surgery ahead of him. Besides, the very first thing that had attracted him to Lizzy was her single-minded focus on becoming the best. She would've spoken up if she'd thought he was being an idiot—just as she had today. Lizzy was nobody's fool—and certainly not his.

He channelled a fresh surge of energy and forced himself to see the infant's body afresh. What could they do to ensure this small, helpless child lived a healthy, happy life?

'How're the oxygen levels?' he asked.

Lizzy's eyes flicked up to the monitor. 'Okay for now. There are spare bloods to hand?'

'*Si.*'

Both of them looked back at the screen, where

the images from the laparoscope showed the delicate workings inside the baby's abdomen.

'There doesn't seem to be any damage here, which is good. The drainage system seems to have kept the area clear of infection.'

'Risky for a little tyke under a thousand grams.'

He glanced up and met her eyes. Was that an accusation?

But her head was nodding in the way it did when she was bowled over by something— impressed.

'How much bowel do you think was compromised?' she asked after they'd removed the laparoscope and closed the microscopic incision.

It was a weighted question. Would Luca need ongoing healthcare? Would it last beyond his infancy or would this surgery set him up for a lifetime of never needing to know any of this had happened?

He watched her precise stitching and delicate tying of the surgical knot. The external scar, if there was one, would be no larger than a freckle.

Is she thinking of our own child when she makes each stitch? Ties each knot?

Leon was. Their own child's health. Its care.

Its development. All the thoughts he should've slammed in a box were now charging each surgical move he made.

'You're opting for an external incision for the bowel removal?' Lizzy asked.

Again he looked up to see if it was a challenge.

But her eyes, when he met them, only held interest.

Not everything's a dare, Leon. Not everything's a move in a chess game.

Competition for that number one spot had fuelled them back in the day. Had she softened in that respect? Or, more likely, grown confident enough not to need to peacock her talents in an OR? The main objective was the welfare of the child. Exactly as it should be.

She was, in short, the exceptional professional he'd met and fallen for seven years ago when he thought he knew all there was to know about life.

He gave his head a small, sharp shake and realigned his focus. He began explaining step by step what he'd be doing, and what each of the surgical nurses, anaesthetists and other members of the surgical team would be doing to give the tiny child they had before them the best chance of survival.

Lizzy was her usual inquisitive self, but clearly she was refusing to showboat about the identical surgeries that he knew for a fact she'd done.

She was a picture-perfect surgical companion. She was always there to provide the second pair of hands when needed. Was waiting, needle poised, prepared to make an exact stitch wherever one was required without needing a prompt. It was a critical timesaver as, so often in surgery, timing was of the utmost importance.

Had their relationship been as easy? Had it even been a relationship? Neither of them had ever referred to the other as their partner.

An uncomfortable feeling that it might have been that simple teased at the back of his mind. He silenced it. Now wasn't the time to dwell on the past.

'Ooh!' Lizzy gave a quiet cheer when, twenty minutes later, he moved his hands back to let her take a look. 'Looks like the bowel is clear of all necrotic tissue and this little fella stands a good chance of a happy, normal life.'

They looked at one another, and he saw the crinkles by her eyes showing the smile her surgical mask was hiding. They'd deepened since their time together back in New York. As had the furrow between her brow.

'*Bravo, Dottore,*' she said.

'*Brava, Dottore,*' he echoed, trying not to betray the hint of sadness he felt that he hadn't been around to see the subtle, sweet changes in her face over the years.

Instead, he gave his usual brisk, efficient instructions about moving Luca back to the NICU and said that he'd be in shortly to have a look. Then he nodded towards the swinging doors that led to the private room where Luca's parents were no doubt biting their nails, waiting for news of their son.

As he walked alongside Lizzy it struck him afresh how fragile the lives of his tiny patients were. Obviously he knew it on a pragmatic level—saving those lives was at the very essence of his profession. But the woman who was carrying his child had just helped him perform surgery on a thirty-week-old baby, pushing aside the fact that what was happening to Luca, or to any of the other infants struggling for survival here in the NICU, might happen to theirs.

He was going to have to plumb the depths of the same strength if he wanted to make good on his promise to be there for their child. He was going to have to do a lot of things if he was going to give his child the best start in life.

CHAPTER SEVEN

'COFFEE?'

As Lizzy came out of her room Leon was already busy at his espresso machine, going through what was clearly a well-rehearsed morning ritual. His elegant surgeon's hands spooned coffee into a paper disc, then cinched the filter into place so that the hot steamed water could do its magic.

'No, thanks.' Lizzy dragged a comb through her shower-wet hair. 'I'm caffeine-free now, remember.'

Their eyes caught and her comb paused midjourney. He held up a tin of decaffeinated coffee. Of course he'd remembered. The shadows under his eyes were proof that at least one of the two of them had been up half the night, remembering and making changes, preparing... Unlike Lizzy, who had slept like a baby.

'That was nice, last night.'

To an outsider, the comment might have appeared to be in reference to a night of passion.

'I can't believe I'd forgotten how precise your stitches were.' He raised his small espresso cup in a toast, then drank.

'Are,' she corrected playfully, pleased Leon's mind had gone exactly where hers had. The surgical ward.

Maybe this whole having a baby and working together for the next few months would work out. Somehow. Not the marriage part, obviously. Leon had clearly had a common-sense malfunction somewhere between his heart and his cerebral cortex. An information overload that had forced an old-fashioned response to a not so old-fashioned situation.

Although...

Her thoughts returned to that single, heartfelt admission: *I don't want to be alone when I live.*

The Leon she'd thought she knew would never have admitted as much. Maybe losing his mother really had changed him. Losing her own mum had certainly changed her. But in the opposite way. It had made her less willing to consider a relationship. Less willing to trust a man's intentions. Less willing to believe

Leon Cassanetti had meant it when he'd proposed marriage.

As such, she'd not brought it up again after they'd returned from the hospital and they'd each—a bit awkwardly, a bit hastily—shut themselves behind the doors of their own very separate bedrooms.

Hopefully the next two or three months would follow a pattern. They'd go to work, do their jobs, find some sort of happy middle ground wherein he acknowledged that it was for the best that she raise her child—*their* child—on her own and then, when the little one was old enough, she would come over here and meet the other half of the gene pool.

Baby daddy? No. Gene pool made him easier to keep at arm's length emotionally. Gene pool it was.

She couldn't help but give him a quick scan. *Mmm...* It was a most excellent gene pool. Theirs was a lucky baby.

'Ten minutes enough before we set off?' Leon asked, his lightly accented voice sending too obvious a physical response through her body.

Gene pool. Gene pool. Gene pool!

'Scooter again?' She mimed putting on her helmet.

He shook his head. 'I thought we'd walk. I'll give you a mini-tour of Rome.'

Twenty minutes later it was taking all of Lizzy's self-discipline not to lace her fingers through Leon's. It wasn't just that their hands kept brushing as they moved in closer together on the pavement to let others pass, it was the sheer romance of the city.

Rome was everything she'd dreamt it might be. Like stepping into a postcard and having it smell and look exactly the way she'd thought it would. Fast and slow-paced all at the same time. Infused with a heavenly golden light. With scents of bitter coffee and sweet pastries wafting out on street corners as shopkeepers opened up for a day's business.

Taking a different route from the one they had on the scooter, Leon guided her through a glorious procession of high-end fashion boutiques nestled alongside centuries' old churches where women dressed all in black ducked in and out for their morning prayers as easily as they did the scrumptious-looking delicatessens and vegetable shops.

Produce you'd never find in a supermarket back home was presented in sumptuous piles:

courgette flowers with baby vegetables attached, fresh, succulent artichokes, and a green vegetable she couldn't identify.

'What's that?' She pointed to the display of long, slender strands fashioned into a green wreath-like heart.

Leon smiled. *'Agretti.* It's... Do you know samphire? A sea vegetable? I think you call it saltwort.'

Lizzy laughed. 'I think I prefer *agretti* as a name.'

Leon signalled to the shop owner that they would take some. 'They also call it *barbe di frate*—friar's beard.' He stroked an invisible space below his own clean-shaven chin, grinning as the shopkeeper handed him a small brown bag full of the vegetable. 'We'll have it tonight with supper. Perhaps get some fresh seafood on the way home.' He held up the bag. 'The *agretti* are only in season a short time, so it is special that you're here for it.'

She bit down on the inside of her cheek to stop herself from saying it would be special to be here at any time of year because of her tour guide. She had no idea how, but because of him the city already felt familiar to her.

She'd obviously need a map if left to her own devices, but it was as if all the stories he'd told her about his home city had become a part of her. If she'd had a free hour to wander about, she wouldn't have felt anything but happy, knowing that familiar surprise after surprise waited around each corner. The Trevi Fountain and the Spanish Steps appeared as old friends sometimes did—unexpected but no less wonderful for it—and by the time they reached the hospital, fortified with two bags of pastries for a mid-morning snack which, of course, she had already sampled, she had to force her work hat back on.

Today and all the days that would follow were about ensuring the conjoined twins came into the world healthy and ready for the separation surgery that would follow. Then, when that had happened, she hoped she'd know exactly what was happening with her own baby. Or, more to the point, the role Leon would play in her baby's life.

After they'd changed into scrubs Leon took her on his morning rounds, with that same energy buzzing between them as when they'd practically raced to the surgery board each morning in New York, to see who was working on what and, more importantly, if they'd be doing it together.

They visited patient after patient, their energies concentrated on the all-important task of ensuring they gave each woman and the baby growing inside her the very best start in life possible.

Pre-eclampsia. Gestational diabetes. Hyper-emis gravidarum—the intense morning sickness that had made headlines when Britain's future Queen had fallen victim to it. There were countless things that could go wrong with a pregnancy but, Lizzy reminded herself with a soft touch to her own belly, countless things that went right.

It was actually a genuine joy to watch Leon at work. He was like an energy bomb, infusing each mum-to-be with a confidence and comfort, telling her that her number one job was to relax. His job was to find solutions. And that was precisely what he would do.

They spoke with a woman who'd been admitted the previous day suffering from heavy blood-loss owing to placenta previa.

'You've had a blood transfusion and a steroid injection, *si*?' Leon asked her.

The woman, Valentina, gave a heavy nod.

'The nurse this morning said all I needed now was rest. So...' Her eyes pinged between Leon and Lizzy, as if she was unsure whose sympathies to play on the most. She ended with a small bat of her eyelashes in Leon's direction. 'I guess you could sign me out?'

Leon tipped his head from side to side—another familiar gesture that Lizzy had somehow let grow fuzzy as the years had passed. It said a thousand things at once. *You're right. There are other sides to that coin. I want you to have the best information I can give you so you can make a well-informed decision.*

'True,' he said. 'You do need rest. But because of the blood-loss and the Braxton Hicks you were experiencing yesterday, it'd be safer for you to stay with us here. Another blood-loss like that could cause immediate distress to the baby, and being able to respond quickly with all the right equipment and supplies is critical when it comes to such a fragile life. Your life could depend upon it as well.'

He rattled through a few statistics and gave her some solid historical examples of what might happen if she were to experience a similar bleed at her home—which was, according to her chart, a good hour outside of Rome.

'*Per favore,*' the woman pleaded with Leon. 'I can rest better at home. My husband needs me, and being here seems a waste when all I do is sit!'

Leon nodded, taking on board her concerns, and then gently explained—exactly as Lizzy would have—that her blood loss had been severe, and that at only thirty weeks they really would like to give the baby a bit more time to develop. In short, staying in hospital meant she was giving her child the best possible chance of a healthy start in life.

'But isn't it better for me and my baby to be relaxed? How can I relax here, with all this… this…mechanical stuff around me?' Valentina gestured at the monitors and screens flanking her bed. The cart filled with medical equipment prepped for emergencies.

'If you want your husband to bring some things in to make the room more personal, we're more than happy to ring him.'

'I don't want anyone to ring him! I want to go home!' Valentina cried with characteristic Italian passion.

Lizzy smiled. It was clear Valentina was in a happy, enriching marriage and that her safe place was with her husband. Her child's welfare, however, would be best attended to right here at St Nicolino's.

'You.' Valentina pointed at her. 'You're very quiet. You're a doctor and a woman. What would you do if you were in my shoes?'

Lizzy apologised for her stilted use of Italian, took the woman's hand and said truthfully, 'If there was anywhere in the world I could be if I were you I'd be right here.' Avoiding the possibility of more butterflies in her tummy, she kept her gaze away from Leon as she continued. 'Dr Cassanetti prefers patients to be at home if they can be. He's well aware that there is added strain in being here, away from your loved ones, but he's asking you to do it so that you can return to them with your baby, both of you healthy and well.'

Leon caught her eyes, gratitude capturing his features in a way that seemed over the top for what had been her genuine professional opinion. She respected Leon. On a professional level and, begrudgingly, a personal level. They'd never made promises to one another back in New York. Had always been very clear that their number one goals in life were to lead departments in their respective countries. And now they did that. Job done.

So…was it possibly time for a new goal?

She forced herself to tune in again as he wrapped up his talk with Valentina, promising to make her stay as comfortable as possible. When they'd left the room he said nothing, but shot Lizzy another look. One that felt complicit…as if they now shared a secret mission. Her spine tingled in response. A sensation, she realised, that would only grow as they began to work with the conjoined twins.

Trying not to stare directly, she kept on throwing Leon secret little glances as they made their way to the next room. Was he experiencing it, too? This jolt of shared connection that felt more like a muscle memory than something new? Was it too dangerous to recapture? she wondered? That feeling of togetherness? She'd felt invincible when they were a team. As if anything in the world was possible so long as they were together.

Leon stopped outside a private room and tapped on his tablet for a moment. When he looked up again, that hard-won smile of his was in place. 'You'll find this one interesting.'

'Oh?'

'Mmm…' He kept his voice low as he explained. 'Maria Paloma. Came in two days ago for a twenty-five-week scan and we discovered ABS.'

'Amniotic Band Syndrome?'

'*Sì.*'

Lizzy instinctively swept her hands to the slight curve of her belly. So slight it might easily be mistaken for a large breakfast. She glanced into the room, only able to catch sight of the woman's swollen belly and her hands rubbing it over and over, as if for good luck. ABS was rare, but in this day and age, if it was caught early enough and treated by an excellent team of surgeons, it was something that didn't have to cause the profound trauma to an unborn child it once had.

'How bad?' She was, as Leon would know, asking after the fibrous, string-like pieces of tissue which had become detached from the amniotic sack and entangled the baby. This tissue, if attached to the growing child, would restrict blood flow and in some extreme cases cause stunted bone growth and even in utero amputation.

'Some of the bands are attached to the cheek.'

Lizzy's lips thinned to a wince. 'Risk of cleft palate?'

'High. I don't think it was caught early enough. We've informed our plastics team. They'll ensure any malformation is minimal. But at this stage it's always hard to say.'

There was regret in his features, as there always had been when he knew a child would have to go through a surgical trauma before its life outside the womb even began.

But that was life, she supposed. A struggle for survival from the very first day. Was it easier when you were part of a team? Knowing you had someone to lean on when the weight became too much? In other words, the total opposite of her parents' marriage where it had been fight or submit. Her father had always been more than happy to point out that there might be no 'I' in team…but there was an 'm' and an 'e' and as such that made him the boss.

'Lizzy?'

Leon was looking at her inquisitively. As if for just a second he'd caught a glimpse of something of her life she'd not let him have access to when they'd been together.

A part of her crumbled. There was no chance she could consider marrying someone she didn't know and who, more to the point, she hadn't trusted to know her. The *real* her.

Leon waved a hand in front of her face. 'Lizzy? *Buongiorno!* Are you feeling a bit of jet lag?'

She shook her head, unwilling to admit that she'd been raking over the past when she should have been focussing on the future.

Leon's forehead creased with concern. 'Maybe we should find you an on-call room before our meeting with Dr Lombardi and the Bianchis, so you can have a rest? I'm happy to finish the rounds on my own.'

She shook her head again, and gave what she hoped was a light-hearted laugh, feeling her topknot loosen into a very messy bun as she did. *Work.* Work was the one thing they could talk about without any sort of additional angst. That was what she would focus on for now.

'Any sign of the bands tightening on the umbilical cord?'

Leon's features sobered. 'No, thank goodness. Just the cheek, so the baby's getting all the nutrition it needs. I'll be in surgery this afternoon, if you'd like to join me?'

'Absolutely.' She gave him a play punch on the arm. 'You didn't think I flew all the way over here just to be a pretty face on the sidelines, did you?'

His expression clouded for a moment and then, as if he'd made a decision, cleared. For the first time since she'd arrived Leon looked exactly like the man she'd told herself she'd fallen in love with all those years ago. Intense, keenly passionate about his work, and *present* in a way few people could be. All his energies were trained on her, and with that came a heated rush of exhilaration. A spine-tingling energy that coursed through her as the world around her faded.

'Lizzy you are one of the most exacting, fearless antenatal surgeons in the world. That's why I wanted you to be part of my team. These conjoined twins deserve the very best, and as far as I'm concerned you are at the top of that list. Do not discredit yourself by even suggesting you're here to decorate the place.'

He waited until she gave him a nod to acknowledge the compliment. Not, she knew, because he wanted recognition for being so magnanimous, but because he wanted her to champion herself.

Even in the highly charged, ego-fuelled environment of surgical internships, where one surgery could make or break your career, Lizzy had never been comfortable tooting her own horn. Her father had drilled into her his belief that modesty was the only attribute a woman should fully embrace. That, and loyalty. In her mother's case, a loyalty fuelled by fear.

'If you want to join in any of my surgeries you are more than welcome,' Leon continued. He briefly broke his gaze, glancing over her shoulder as if, like her, he'd suddenly become aware of the people around them. He lowered his voice and said, 'I also appreciate you coming over for the personal reason. It was a brave thing to do.'

Lizzy's heart-rate accelerated yet again. Work talk she could do. But baby talk…? She'd thought they were going to shelve that for now. They had to. Until she knew exactly what was going on between the two of them and that would take time.

She hastily told the part of herself that knew the two were inextricably linked to be quiet. 'Maybe we can talk about that later?'

Leon fixed her with a solid look. 'Do you want to know why I asked you over here?'

She gave him a side-on look. 'You just said. The conjoined twins, right?'

'They were the excuse, but they weren't the reason.'

He reached out and tucked a tendril of loose hair behind her ear, his fingertips tracing down the length of her neck. It was a gesture that elicited far too many inappropriate memories. Memories she had vowed to consign to the past.

His fingers lingered just that infinitesimal bit longer than they should have. And when his eyes met hers she felt as though her body had finally, at long last, found the energy source it had been seeking for so long. Her heart bashed against her ribcage. Was this Leon's way of telling her he had actual genuine feelings for her? This was definitely not what she'd bargained on when she'd boarded the plane.

She must have stood there, blinking at him like an idiot, to the point when he felt she needed help. Because, with a hand on her elbow, he began to steer her towards an on-call room. 'Lizzy, there's something I think you need to know—'

'Ah! Leon. Just the man I was looking for!'

Leon's body language instantly shifted from doting father-to-be about to bare his soul to briskly efficient surgeon. Instead of relief, she felt a hit of loss that she might never know what Leon had been about to tell her.

'Giovanni. I'd like to introduce you to—'

'No need,' said the handsome doctor, tapping the side of his nose with a mischievous smile. 'I know all about Dr Beckley.'

CHAPTER EIGHT

LEON IGNORED LIZZY'S lightning-fast glare.

'It sounds like something other than my professional reputation precedes me,' Lizzy said, smiling and giving Giovanni's hand a shake.

'Nothing that wouldn't add to your accolades,' said Giovanni charmingly. 'How could one work in our business and *not* know about the world-famed Baby Heart Doctor Elizabeth Beckley?'

Lizzy gave Leon another look, this one saying, *What exactly have you told this man?*

She let go of Giovanni's hand. 'Sounds like you already know who I am. And you are…?'

'Giovanni Lombardi.'

Leon was about to jump in and apologise for his lack of manners, for not making a formal introduction and for his absence of brain power, but he was still trying to regroup from having been almost caught steering Lizzy into an on-call room, where he would have been dangerously close to repeating his foolhardy proposal.

The words were banging round his head. He *loved* her. It was a hell of an epiphany. He'd finally admitted to himself that he loved this woman and had done from back in those days in New York. He wasn't single these days by choice. He was single because he loved the woman he'd arrogantly and ignorantly let slip through his fingers five years ago.

He didn't want to let it happen again. Perhaps his next proposal should be more thought-out. Now was his chance to change history. It would be messy. No doubt about that. He was a gifted bachelor, but he'd do everything in his power to make sure she knew he was going to change. Somehow.

What sort of evidence would she need? A diamond? A public declaration? Learning how to sing opera? No. She'd see right through those gestures for what they would be. Disingenuous. None of them were *him*, apart from the diamond, but his gut told him that with her colouring she was more of a sapphire girl.

Oh, Dio. That was a whole new rabbit hole he could disappear in. The whole point of Lizzy being here was to concentrate, not become a ring expert!

After a few more easily rejected ideas, he forced himself to tune in to a discussion that was in full flow.

'Amazing! Though I have to say with his track record I'm not surprised,' Lizzy was saying.

'Absolutely. A stroke of genius. Leon's ability to look beyond the obvious is exemplary.'

She threw him a quick, inquisitive look, clearly impressed by whatever it was she and Giovanni were talking about.

As he was completely clueless, and didn't want to betray the fact that he hadn't been listening, Leon put on what he hoped was a modest expression and gave them a benign smile. 'It was nothing, really.'

'It was innovative. Well,' Giovanni qualified, 'it was ancient. But it was an innovation we wouldn't have thought of if Leon hadn't put it forward.'

'Who would've thought it? Honey! I'm impressed.' Lizzy gave Leon an admiring smile then turned back to Giovanni. 'Is it available elsewhere in the world?' Lizzy asked, looking truly interested.

He wished like hell he knew what they were

talking about. And why was Lizzy calling him 'honey' in front of his boss? He'd thought they'd agreed to keep things professional here.

'Leon?' Giovanni prompted. 'It's available elsewhere, isn't it?'

Leon gave a cautious nod. 'In some areas…' He hoped that was true. Certain medical supplies or treatments would be difficult to offer in, say, Antarctica. Then again, he hadn't invented any medical supplies. His mind reeled, trying to catch up.

'Nonsense!' Giovanni cut in. 'You know as well as I do that it's available everywhere. It's just that not everyone sees medicine the way you do. A true Leonardo da Vinci, our Leon.'

'Hey!' Lizzy clapped. 'That's what I used to call him. Da Vinci. Ha! A visionary with a flow chart.'

Giovanni rocked back on his heels and roared with laughter. '*Oh, Dio!* That's him, all right. He likes to dot his "i"s and cross his "t"s—don't you Leon?'

Giovanni gave him a clap on the shoulder that felt strangely like a prompt to laud his own merits.

Lizzy laughed appreciatively. 'That's definitely the Leon I know.'

She started telling Giovanni about one of the first surgeries they performed together. Leon had made massive wall charts of the entire innovative surgery and posted them around the walls of the operating theatre, so that everyone had quite literally been on the same page as they'd changed a child's life for the better.

Giovanni laughed along with her, saying that sounded just like the Leon he knew as well, and adding that his fastidiousness was one of the many reasons they had wanted him to head the antenatal unit at St Nicolino's. Did Lizzy know he headed the department? he asked.

She gave him a punch on the arm. 'You didn't tell me that.'

He forced a modest smile to come into play again. *What was going on here?*

Giovanni shook his head and said that he hoped while Lizzy was there she'd teach their cherished Dr Cassanetti a thing or two about sharing his genius in the world's medical journals, as she had done.

Lizzy's smile softened as her eyes lit on him. 'I'll do my best. He has a way of seeing the world that's…extraordinary.'

'Yes, he does,' said Giovanni, dropping a duplicitous wink in Leon's direction before drawing Lizzy's attention back to him. 'And I think you're just the woman to make sure he sees that for himself!'

Suddenly it occurred to him what was happening. Giovanni Lombardi was *flirting* on his behalf. Or—wait! His heart jammed in his throat. *Had Lizzy told Giovanni she was pregnant with his child?*

No. She wouldn't have done that. Not without checking with him.

Giovanni gave Lizzy a courtly bow. 'It's absolutely lovely to meet you, Dr Beckley. I can't tell you how grateful we are that you've joined us here at St Nicolino's. I look forward to spending more time with you.'

All right. No need to slather on the gratitude, Leon grumbled silently. Protectively. *Very* protectively.

Giovanni threw a discreet look over Lizzy's shoulder at Leon. A look that said very clearly, *Now I see why you've been so distracted.*

'Shall we…?' Giovanni gestured towards a small lecture theatre where they had agreed to meet the entire team and discuss the conjoined twins.

'Absolutely!' Leon said, a tad too enthusiastically.

As they entered the room Lizzy gave him a nudge in the ribs and blew out a low whistle of approval. 'Honey... Who would've thought it? Well, you did, obviously.'

What was she *talking* about? And, again, since when did Lizzy call him 'honey'?

And then he twigged. Giovanni had been talking about his idea to put medical grade honey around prematurely born infant's feeding tubes as an antidote to extravasation injuries—wounds that sometimes struggled to heal. *Let the honey do the healing*—that had been his tagline when he'd first tried out the ancient remedy, for its antimicrobial and wound-healing properties.

He forced his nervous system to cool its jets. Not everything was about him and Lizzy. Well... Yes, it was. Because as they entered the room a twenty-strong team of medical professionals rose and, as one, applauded their entrance as if they were royalty.

An hour later he was back on much stronger footing. Science. Medicine. One very specific goal.

'And that is how we see the procedure going from our end—pending, of course, any complications. We are a team, Dr Beckley and I.

Think of us as one unit. Keeping Baby A well on a cardiovascular level is critical to both of the Bianchi babies' welfare—and, of course, their mother's. If you have any questions at any time about the Bianchis you come to either of us. We are one.'

He pressed his two fingers together so that the group could see that he really meant it. His eyes shot to Lizzy's. It was a speech he regularly gave whenever he worked with a visiting physician, but the language felt more potent when it was about Lizzy.

Lizzy cocked an eyebrow at him. *We?* it was saying. *One unit?*

The Lizzy he'd worked with five years ago had loved working with him as a unit. This Lizzy, for some reason, looked really annoyed.

'Dr Beckley and I will, of course, be keeping you updated in advance of the surgery. That's it for now. *Grazie mille*, everyone. Let's make this a sure-fire success so that Dr Lombardi and his team—as yet to be announced—will have two healthy babies when the time comes.'

Lizzy waited until the crowd of doctors who had swarmed around Leon to ask questions specific to their own roles had eased. Some of the team had, very kindly, taken the time to introduce themselves to her. She had never known there were so many Marias in the world!

She made a mental note to ask Leon for a cheat sheet later, so she could tell them all apart. Nothing made a surgical team work better than genuinely feeling like a team. Knowing everyone's name without having to look at their name tag was the easiest place to start. And another factor that made a team work was feeling included in the decision-making. Something she hadn't yet felt on this case. Sure, she'd only been here twenty-four hours, but…

She was used to being in charge of her own team—not following someone else's lead. Particularly when the 'leader' was a certain someone who was yanking her emotions hither and yon. *Marry me. Don't marry me. Let's be a family. Let's not be a family.*

Okay. Perhaps he hadn't said some of those things, but it felt as if he had, and that surely had to mean her gut was trying to tell her something, right?

But what, exactly?

Lizzy sighed. Maybe this up, down, all around stretchy emotional boundaries thing was what all the expectant mothers who burst into tears for no reason in the tinned vegetable aisle at the supermarket were talking about. She wasn't feeling weepy, though. She was feeling cross. *Very* cross. Which didn't make sense.

The logical part of her brain knew Leon was a fortnight ahead of her on the project, so of course he'd given the introductory lecture. But the part of her brain that had received a marriage proposal and that knew she was as good a surgeon as he was, shook with anxiety that this might be what life with Leon would be like. Taking a back seat to his opinion, no matter what she had to say. Just like her mother had done with her father.

She tried to shake some common sense back into her body.

It's his hospital, dummy! He's the MFMS. Of course he's taking the lead! He's also lauded you as critical to the twins' survival! The last thing he's doing is sidelining you. He's trying to include you, not exclude you.

Grr! Feelings. They were annoying when you didn't want them.

The part of her that wasn't a raging torrent of hormones knew for a fact that her time that day would've been better spent studying the case, not following him on his rounds like a lovesick puppy. She looked up at him, still standing on the small lecture hall stage, with staff gathered round him as if he were a superstar. Which he kind of was. Who wouldn't be with those looks and a brain like his? And the things that man could do with his hands...

She looked away, her body responding a little too viscerally to the mere suggestion of his touch. Maybe if she saw him every day the tingles would fade...or maybe she should have sex with Leon while she was here? Just to properly get him out of her system.

'Lizzy!' Leon appeared before her, his eyes bright with anticipation. 'So! What did you think?' He clapped his hands together and gave them a good rub, his eyes glinting brightly, the way they always had when a particularly complicated case presented itself.

'Nice presentation, Dr Cassanetti,' she said crankily, to disguise the fact that she had just been thinking of him naked and in an extremely compromising position.

'Thanks, I think...?'

'No, seriously.' Her clipped tone was making it entirely clear that she was annoyed. 'It was kind of you to make it look as though I actually know what's going on, but if you remember I haven't actually met the patients yet. A bit dangerous, wasn't it, to announce that I'm going to help make this operation "a sure-fire success"?'

Leon threw a look over his shoulder, as if he expected some sort of reason for her mood-change to appear before him. He looked back at her, more warily this time. 'What do you mean? You've done this kind of operation dozens of times before.'

'Not on a conjoined twin with a shared aortic valve.' She gave him a knowing look, indicating that it wasn't wise to make promises you weren't sure you could keep. Like, for example, proposing marriage when you didn't want to be married.

Or did he…?

Pregnancy hormones, Lizzy was beginning to realise, could quickly become exhausting.

'Hey. Where's this coming from? You're an excellent surgeon.'

Leon reached out to touch her arm, but she pulled it back before he could touch her. She could see what he was thinking. That it wasn't like her to be insecure. And he would be right. She wasn't. She was a strong, independent, very happy, not to mention incredibly well-adjusted woman, who didn't need the most gorgeous man in the universe, whose child she happened to be carrying, to make her feel better.

So she proved it by acting normal. She popped on a bright smile and said, 'I'd really like to meet the parents. See a scan. Earn the kudos you gave me, yeah?'

Leon held his arm out towards the doors to the ward. 'After you, m'lady.'

There, thought Lizzy, the smile on her face broadening as she swanned in front of him, *that's more like it!*

'Ooh, there they are!' Lizzy smiled in wonder as she ran the scanning wand over Gabrielle's stomach, all her wild emotions from just moments ago forgotten. This was what she loved. Seeing tiny little lives starting out in the world.

'It *does* look like they're hugging doesn't it?' Gabrielle asked, her eyes flitting between the screen and her husband.

Everyone agreed—it did look as if the girls were hugging. Lizzy guessed that warm thought added a level of comfort to what must be a terrifying experience for both Gabrielle and her husband Matteo. There were a lovely couple. She was from Switzerland and had, on a work secondment, met and married Matteo, who lived in Northern Italy. They'd both come to Rome on their doctor's advice, when they'd made the discovery about their babies.

A thick tumble of ebony curls cascaded over Gabrielle's shoulders, framing features softened by her advancing pregnancy. She was both frightened and brave. Stoic and nervous. Matteo, thankfully, was a picture-perfect doting husband. Holding her hand, checking she was warm enough, not too cold, not thirsty, or hungry, in need of a foot rub…

It made Lizzy smile. It also made her a little jealous, seeing the easy love they shared. They were a couple well and truly devoted to one another's happiness. What confidence that must take, she thought. To trust and believe in someone never to hurt you.

She glanced at Leon, then just as quickly looked away. History was powerful, and the reason it repeated itself was because people didn't learn from it. She didn't want to be one of those people.

She cleared her throat and focused on the screen. 'Shall we take a little look at…? Ooh… look there. Ten little toes on Baby A—'

'Oh, *scusi*!' Matteo interrupted her. 'We're not

calling them Baby A and Baby B any more, if that's all right.'

Lizzy turned away from the screen, giving them both her full attention. 'Absolutely. What would you prefer?'

'Grace and Hope,' Gabrielle said, taking hold of her husband's hand.

'Beautiful names.' Lizzy smiled, her eyes catching Leon's as he concurred with a soft, *'Bellissima...'*

Collectively, they went back to the screen, taking the baby anatomy tour—or, as Lizzy liked to call it, head, shoulders, knees and toes. Lizzy loved this part of being an antenatal doctor. Showing a couple their child, the heartbeat...or in this case the one shared heartbeat. It sounded romantic, an ideal to strive for, but in this case it could prove lethal.

Had that been the problem with her parents' marriage? They hadn't been able to survive without the other? Divorce had never been discussed—and yet her father's powerful heartbeat had seemed to dominate her mother's more fragile, birdlike rhythm. The way he'd said things like 'That's the way we see things—isn't that right, Genny?' or 'We're not interested,' or any number of things her father had decided on behalf of both of them gave Lizzy a cold chill down her spine to this day.

She glanced again at Leon, who had moved to the far end of the bed, having turned things over to her once he'd made the initial introduction. Perhaps he'd read her mood. Realised she'd felt put on the back foot by having to meet the medical team without having so much as met the parents yet. Or perhaps, like her father—and this was a scary thought—she was a control freak.

She stuffed that thought into a box and squirted a whole load of mental superglue all over the lid.

The easy part of the 'tour' was done. Now it was time for trickier terrain. The conjoined chests and hearts.

Lizzy pointed towards the arrow on the sonogram. 'Dr Lombardi and his team will work out how best to approach the separation surgery, but if you look at the arrow, this little spot here is where Hope's and Grace's hearts are fused together.'

Gabrielle gave a little cry of despair.

Lizzy took her hand and gave it a gentle squeeze. 'You have got the very best medical team in the world at your disposal.'

'And you've done this surgery before? The HLHS?'

'Absolutely. Many times.'

'On conjoined twins?'

Lizzy shook her head. 'This is a first. But I know the surgery inside and out, and the aortic valve the twins share shouldn't change the standard procedure. If anything, it should enable their hearts to work better together up until the separation surgery.'

'There's a standard procedure for this sort of thing?' Matteo's eyes widened.

'Absolutely. I know having conjoined twins is a rarity, but one in four thousand babies is diagnosed with HLHS. There are specialised units around the world to help, and one of them is right here.'

'But you're not from here. Should we have gone to Sydney instead?' The couple shared an anxious look.

Lizzy could feel Leon's eyes on her, but he didn't jump in and make a case for his hospital. Interesting… He really was doing his best to show her he trusted her.

'This is the best place for the two of you. The *four* of you,' she corrected herself with a laugh. 'You're as close to home as you can be and, thanks to the hospital's facilities for parents, you don't have to be parted. Being together during your pregnancy is the very best thing you two can do to keep yourself happy. Those babies will feel your love. Your strength.'

She kept her eyes firmly on the Bianchis, vividly aware that she'd pretty much said the exact opposite to Leon.

What was it her father had used to say? *Do as I say, not as I do?*

The thought lurched uncomfortably close to the child in her own belly.

Tapping her pen officiously on her knee, she continued, 'Any specialist hospital will have a team of brilliant surgeons and physicians. This one is no exception. The fact that I'm here is—'

Foolishly, she looked at Leon. In the microsecond of eye contact they shared she finally believed him when he'd said he hadn't invited her here for the surgery. Well, obviously he had—but the real reason ran much deeper.

'I don't want to live my life alone!'

She tore her eyes away and put on her sensible doctor's voice. 'We've got around forty people dedicated to supporting you through this pregnancy, with Dr Cassanetti helming the ship as it were. And after the babies are born Dr Lombardi will literally have dozens of highly specialised medical staff ready and waiting to help your two little girls to the best of their ability.'

Lizzy felt but did not see Leon pressing himself up to his full height as she talked the couple through the Hypoplastic Left Heart Syndrome surgery. They nodded, asked questions, stopped and doubled back when they didn't understand something.

Given the fact she'd just bitten his head off for making promises he couldn't keep, she knew she was standing on thin ice when she wrapped up the consultation by saying, 'We will do everything we can, Dr Cassanetti and I, to make sure Hope and Grace have the very best start in life.'

'But what if that start instantly comes with problems?' Gabrielle sniffed and, unsurprisingly, tears began to slip down her cheeks.

Lizzy startled herself by saying. 'That's life, isn't it? It's full of risks. Which ones do we take? Which ones do we leave for the more foolhardy? Or, more to the point, which ones do we regret not taking?' She smiled at the couple, who had to be so frightened. 'I know the surgeries Dr Cassanetti and I perform come with a long list of potential problems, but we humans are a pretty resilient bunch. We're able to separate the bright side from the dark side and focus on the one that's going to bring the better outcome.'

It was a statement 'old Leon' would've billed as psychological poppycock, but she caught him nodding out of the corner of her eye, murmuring *'Si...'* and *'Absolutely...'* as the Bianchis pulled them in for hugs of gratitude for their attention and care.

When it was Leon's turn to be caught in a fierce hug from Gabrielle, he looked over her shoulder and caught Lizzy's gaze with his own.

'Some risks *are* worth taking, aren't they?' he said.

And she knew he was talking about their future when he continued.

'I believe this is one of them. Don't you, Dr Beckley?'

CHAPTER NINE

'*BUONGIORNO.*' LEON KNOCKED on the doorframe of the hospital on-call room where, once again, Lizzy had spent the night on the premise of 'monitoring' Gabrielle's babies.

It was a job the overnight staff were well-equipped to do, and they were, of course, under strict instructions to ring either of them the moment they sensed trouble. It looked as if he wasn't the only ostrich who stuck its head in the sand—or, in this case, in the antenatal unit—when there were personal problems to confront...

'Oh, my God, you're an angel.' Lizzy grabbed the coffee, then flashed him a questioning smile. 'Decaf?'

'Obviously.'

'Pistachio?' she asked, already taking a bite of the flaky pastry he knew she favoured.

'*Si,*' he confirmed, enjoying watching her devour the pastry, and then another.

This had been how they'd done things since that first day of working together. She'd insist she needed to stay at the hospital to get a proper grasp of the overall medical situation with the Bianchis, and would send him home with a promise that she'd use the spare key he'd given her. The next day, her bed untouched, he'd find her, courtesy of a nurse, in an on-call room, either asleep or poring over case files. They would go over her thoughts, meet with Giovanni after they'd checked in on Gabrielle and the twins, and then he'd go on his rounds. Sometimes with her. Sometimes without her.

He knew better than to push, because he didn't like to be pushed either—and if he was the pot she was the kettle. In other words, it took a control freak to know one. Neither of them liked having matters taken out of their own hands, and that was precisely what having a child together did. Because life wasn't just about 'me, myself and I' any more. It was about 'us' and 'we' and 'it'. 'It', of course, being the baby, which would require changing and feeding and cuddling during bouts of late-night crying. Elements of life he'd never thought would be a part of his own.

Lizzy yawned and stretched, pressing her

hands to her lower back, and then glared at the on-call bed. 'They could do with slightly comfier mattresses here.'

'You *can* sleep at the flat, you know,' Leon said, although an image of her tangled in his bedsheets inconveniently popped into his mind.

She barely glanced at him, but her thoughts had clearly gone in the same direction his had because her cheeks coloured. The only times that happened was when she was thinking saucy thoughts or when she was fuming—and she definitely wasn't fuming.

'I know,' she said. 'I just… I've got a funny feeling.'

Leon rocked back on his heels and nodded. Okay. The Lizzy he'd worked with before hadn't often spoken of feelings dictating her decision-making, but now, pregnancy hormones aside, he'd felt it himself. That kick in the gut that told him something wasn't quite right with a medical situation.

'Do you think we're wrong to wait to do the operation?'

She'd suggested holding back by only a few days, but he knew as well as she did that sometimes life and death hung in the balance of a handful of seconds.

'No, but I...' She hesitated, scrubbing the sleep out of her eyes and then swooping her hair up into a messy and strangely adorable ponytail. 'Yes.' She gave him a solid look as she stood up and then added a foot-stamp. 'I was going over the scans a couple of hours ago—'

'You were up a *couple of hours* ago?'

She shrugged. 'Woke up full of beans, I guess. Then ran out of them. Anyway... Yes, I do think we're wrong to wait. These little girls are facing enough hard work in the womb as it is. Sharing a critical aortic valve means the left side of Hope's heart is having to work that much harder than it already is, and as such I think we should ease the burden. Then again... if it can gain strength on its own that's a plus. Also, the stent that would go in now would be minuscule—not that that's a problem—but...'

She gnawed on the inside of her cheek, hashing through the countless variables that factored into heart surgery for a twenty-three-week-old baby.

Leon leant against the doorframe, enjoying watching Lizzy whirl round the room, picking up her watch, her phone, trying to tie her hair up into a ponytail, again, even though she'd just done it. Even watching her scrub a toothbrush against her teeth was fun. Was it possible to miss something you'd never properly had? A routine?

Sure, they'd spent a lot of time together in New York, but that had been different. They'd been a classic romcom. Two ambitious surgeons battling it out to be the best whilst fighting—and ultimately succumbing to—a fierce mutual attraction.

Back then, they'd always known that whatever it was they'd shared was going to end. Now, with a baby in the picture, there was a real chance—if the pair of them could sort themselves out—that they would be in each other's lives for ever. Scrap that. They'd *have* to sort themselves out. Because their child wasn't going through life without a father. End of.

'Earth to Leon?' Lizzy spat out her toothpaste. 'I'm asking for your professional opinion here. C'mon. What do you think? Am I being paranoid?'

He straightened up. 'A lot of doctors would argue that it'd be better to wait until the babies are born. The fact that Hope has HLHS and a restrictive atrial septal defect could mean waiting until they're delivered—'

'No!' She made a strangled noise of frustration. 'You wouldn't have flown me half-way across the world if you believed that. You wanted this operation.' She turned the full blaze of her aquamarine eyes on him.

Unblinking he replied, 'And you agreed. You also decided that rather than race into an operation, we should wait until you had "the full picture".'

Why was she getting herself tied up in knots about this? She was Hope's doctor. If she thought they should do the operation, they should do it. As a maternal medicine specialist, he was technically Gabrielle's doctor. But as Gabrielle was carrying Hope and Grace he had to make the call, too. And right now he needed to force Lizzy's hand.

'I brought you in because I knew you would know when to operate. It's not my specialty. It's yours.'

Lizzy pursed her lips at him, then whirled round the room doing a very uncharacteristic final check for her belongings. This from a woman who had a photographic memory...

It made him wonder... What were they really talking about here? The Bianchi babies? Or their baby?

He decided to test the theory. 'Lizzy...there

are many doctors who would caution waiting before making a decision.'

'Oh, really?' Lizzy turned indignant. 'Well, "many doctors" aren't me!' She poked herself in the chest and unexpectedly hiccoughed.

They stared at one another in silence for a minute and then, when the intensity of their eye contact began to morph into something else… something verging on a sexual frisson, Lizzy broke contact and began to laugh. 'Oh, goodness. Listen to me. I've lost the plot. I'm going to blame pregnancy hormones. Can I blame pregnancy hormones?'

Leon shrugged amiably. 'All you like—but please do bear in mind we have actual, real patients waiting for you to decide when you want to wheel them into the operating theatre.'

'I know.' She hung her head, that intense burst of energy now humming at a more manageable level. She looked up and met his gaze. 'I think we should do a scan.'

'Sure. I'll book them in. MRI? Echo?'

'No.' She shook her head. 'I'm not talking about the Bianchis. I'm talking about us. You. Me. Before we see the Bianchis.' She glanced at her watch. 'We have half an hour before they're expecting us, and I can't focus any more. Not with this vagueness hanging over everything. I need clarity, then I can proceed.'

It took all his power to bite his tongue. *She* was the only thing standing between vagueness and clarity. He had proposed to her. Offered to shoulder the load. Said he'd let her move in. Move somewhere else. Live in Sydney. Or had he taken it back? They'd definitely agreed to disagree on something.

Hell. She was right. It was a mess, and seeing the baby would definitely push them into making a decision.

Five minutes later, after Lizzy had downed a couple of glasses of water and he'd prepared the scan room, with the door firmly locked, Leon applied gel to the slight arc of Lizzy's belly, then picked up the wand.

'Ready?'

'If you are.' She smiled nervously.

He put the wand to her skin and… '*Oh, Dio. Amore*...look.'

He felt Lizzy's fingers wrap around his wrist as he moved the wand slowly over her belly, and then that magic moment he'd borne witness to for so many couples happened for him. He heard his child's heartbeat for the very first time.

'Hear that?' Lizzy asked.

'*Si.*' It was all he could manage.

He looked at her, and when their eyes met and meshed he felt that same perfect connection he'd felt when they'd first met. She was a kindred spirit. A woman who understood him perfectly because she was the same. Someone who wanted to be judged for what she was now—not who she'd been or where she'd come from, but for the future she hoped for.

Back then it had been all career, career, career.

Had those goals changed?

The pounding in his chest told him the answer.

Yes. Everything had changed.

Lizzy was the first to break eye contact, her eyes darting back to the sonography screen.

'Any guess as to the sex?'

'Too soon,' he answered as if by rote.

She knew as well as he did that physicians could make a rough guess from twelve weeks, but they also both knew it wasn't always an accurate one. When it wasn't necessary to know the sex, and it wasn't blatantly obvious, Leon liked keeping the big reveal until the twenty-week scan, enjoying the surprise along with the patients.

'We could—' she began.

He shook his head. 'No. No blood tests. Unless…?' He moved the wand towards their baby's neck, zooming in on the image so that they could see whether or not there was increased fluid at the base.

'I've already done the nuchal translucency screening. And the blood test,' she said quietly.

Leon cleared an unexpected knot of emotion from his throat. Of course she'd know what he was doing. Checking for Down's Syndrome. Lizzy was only thirty-five, but there was always a risk.

'We're good. The baby's healthy.'

Lizzy sounded as emotional as he felt.

'It's strange when it's happening to you, isn't it?' Leon voiced what he was sure they were both feeling. 'Completely different.'

She nodded, giving her eyes a quick swipe before returning her focus to the screen.

There was so much that wouldn't be a surprise about her pregnancy, given their professions. Without having to say anything, they both knew the baby would weigh about fifteen grams right now. Bones were beginning to form in the arms and legs. The vocal cords would be developing, as would its personality—whether it would suck its thumb, be a kicker or a nodder, when its tiny neck muscles would be strong enough to move the head from side to side.

'Let's keep it a surprise. Until I deliver.'

Her voice softened and her fingers began to stroke his wrist as he gently moved the wand back and forth across the soft, sweet belly he'd covered in passionate kisses just a few short months ago.

The power of what those kisses had culminated in hit him full force. He was going to be a father. It was up to him to decide what kind of father he wanted to be. A runner, like his own father, or a man who honoured the child he had helped create.

'Beautiful, isn't it?' Lizzy asked. 'All those little fingers and toes. And it's a thumb-sucker—look!'

They both smiled and laughed. Their child's hand could clearly be seen at its mouth, thumb in place between its miniature lips.

Leon could only nod, speech defying him. This was literally a picture-perfect baby. And, given their jobs, they knew how precious this news was.

'Should we call it something? You know… like, erm…' She tapped her chin, her eyes still glued to the screen. *'Pompelmo?'*

He laughed. 'What? Grapefruit? You want to call our child *grapefruit*?'

'Well…' She shrugged. 'It's about the right size.'

'So what are we going to call it next week? *Melone?* And the next? *Cantelupo?*'

Lizzy got the giggles. 'Okay, fine. We won't call it anything.'

Her expression suddenly sobered.

'What?'

'We're going to have to choose a name at some point.'

'We?'

'Well… I had thought of calling her Metrodora. Dora for short. Because Metrodora's a bit mean. I mean…if she's girl.'

Leon tipped his head back and forth. 'A Greek physician, eh? You know how us Italians feel about that.'

Lizzy pulled a face. He knew Metrodora wasn't just any old Greek physician. She was the first female physician to write a proper medical text.

'Don't you think it's time to move past of that Roman versus Greek malarkey about who started civilisation?' she said.

'Sure. Happy to. So long as the answer is the Romans,' Leon said playfully. 'How about Trotula? She was the world's first gynaecologist. From right here in Italy. Or Dorotea Bucca. She was a physician *and* a professor. Nice, huh?'

He tried out a few variations of Dorotea. Dorothy. Téa. And, of course, Dora.

'Nope. Sorry. You don't get to choose,' Lizzy snipped, and the hum of shared delight disappeared as if it had been sucked into a black hole. 'Not since you won't be involved.'

Leon's hackles went up. Hormones or not, this wasn't her call. 'And when did we make that decision, exactly?'

'We made it on the day I arrived, remember? When you took back your proposal.'

'Hang on.' He put the wand on the desk beside the exam table and handed her a few paper towels to wipe the gel off her belly. The magic of the moment was completely gone. 'You made me take it back. And if I recall the conversation properly—which I do—I remember saying we'd put decision-making on hold. Not withdraw any offers made in good faith.'

'Ha! See? I *knew* you didn't mean it.' She shook her head and began muttering something to herself.

'I *did* mean it, Lizzy. It's the right thing to do.'

'Yes, but is it the thing you actually *want* to do, Leon? That's what matters here.'

'Hypothetically...' he said, before he could stop himself.

Lizzy's eyebrows shot up and she held him in a fierce glare as she slipped off the table and pulled her scrubs top down over her stomach.

'I think we should go and see the Bianchis now. They'll be expecting us.'

Lizzy was kicking herself over and over again. Why was she being such a pain with Leon?

It didn't take a brain surgeon to answer that one. Or an antenatal cardiologist for that matter.

She was scared. Scared right down to her very essence.

Of *course* she didn't want to do this on her own. She hadn't even known she wanted a baby until a fortnight ago, when she'd stared at that smiley face on the pregnancy test and then, of course, on the five back-up tests she'd done afterwards.

Of *course* she'd love to be all happy families

with the one man in the world who set her on fire in so many ways—intellectually, professionally, sexually...

The 'sexually' part in particular had been driving her mad. She'd met plenty of pregnant women who said all they thought about was sex when they were carrying a baby, and lo and behold she seemed to be one of them. But having sex with Leon was out of the question. Especially as they hadn't decided on their long-term plan of action. Kissing, hugging, caressing and being totally naked with him would be sheer insanity.

That one night of mind-blowing sex they'd shared in January had changed her life for ever. If she were to have two to three more months of mind-blowing sex who knew what would happen? She might say yes to that ridiculously lovely cream-coloured dress she passed every single day when she sneaked out of the hospital for a secret gelato.

So, no way. There was zero chance she was going to go and stay in that flat of his, with him all naked and gorgeous and Italian, with his sexy voice, and super-sexy hands, and his sexy chin and his kiss-me-now lips and—everything. Especially if he smelt of burnt sugar and oranges as he had this morning. It had taken all the power she'd possessed not to rip her top off and beg him to have his wicked way with her when he'd come into the on-call room this morning. That was how big a game her hormones were playing.

Or maybe…her heart?

These questions and a thousand more plagued her as she sat through the morning meeting with Giovanni and his growing team and then went into the Bianchis' room, where they were now.

'Lizzy?' Leon was prompting. 'Gabrielle was just asking why you think another MRI is a good idea.'

He gave her a look that said a thousand things. *I know you're freaked out. I know you're hormonal. I know we have a lot to talk about.* And, more to the point, *I flew you across the world to help these people.*

'Is it really necessary?' Gabrielle's eyes darted between the doctors and her husband. 'I have to confess they're beginning to make me feel a bit claustrophobic.'

Lizzy retrained her attentions to where they should be. On her patient. 'We can get some music in there for you—or maybe an audio-book would help? Matteo, you're also welcome to stay. The way Gabrielle will be situated in the scanner means you could hold her ankle or maybe rub her feet?'

Gabrielle made a *Maybe that would work* face.

Matteo rubbed his hands together and feigned giving a foot-rub. 'Anything to help my good lady wife.'

Gabrielle bit down on her lip, indecision clearly gripping her.

'I don't know… It might be harder to stay still if he's doing something that feels good.'

Lizzy forced herself not to go in for a fist-bump. Gabrielle was preaching to the converted!

Concentrating on Gabrielle and her babies was exactly why she'd been sleeping on the hard-as-rock beds here at the hospital. Was there *no* hospital, no matter how fancy, that had comfy on-call rooms?

Lizzy sat down by Gabrielle's bed and took the young woman's hand in her own. 'You know more than anyone that the babies you're carrying are extra-special. As such, I want to know exactly what's going on before we take any surgical steps—yeah?'

Gabrielle's husband ran a hand through his already messy hair. 'I think we probably would've been happy doing something else extra-special, like…' he looked at his wife and grinned. '…like building the world's largest snowman or eating the most profiteroles in one sitting or swimming in the world's largest cheese fondue.'

'Food! That's what he is always thinking about!'

'How could I not?' he countered in mock horror. 'We're in Rome! Did you know this is the only month of the year you can get *puntarelle*? And *barbe di frate*! Monk's beard! I'd never even heard of it before.'

Lizzy felt Leon tickle her hand with his finger. She batted it away. She couldn't deal with butterfly swoops in her tummy and acting professional at the same time.

Matteo's wife gave him a loving swat, then tugged him down to her to receive a kiss. 'Enough about food. Can we talk about our children?'

He cupped her cheek in his hand, then bent to kiss her again. 'Of course, *amore mio*. I just don't want you to be stressed. And also… I know how much you love trying new food.'

His wife giggled. 'Don't! You'll make me hungry again and I only just ate.'

'Tell me what you want and I'll fetch it. Your wish is my command.'

The couple shared a warm look of such undiluted shared purpose that a sharp blast of loneliness shot through Lizzy so powerfully she could hardly draw a breath.

She looked away and caught Leon's eye. Instantly that feeling of solitude switched to something powerful and charged. She could be with this man if she wanted. He'd asked her to marry him and there was a kernel of belief in her that he actually had meant it.

Granted, there were a whole load of 'ifs' attached. If she learnt to trust that he wasn't going to be like her father. If he didn't lay down his word as law. And if, the scariest of all, he didn't behave like 'old Leon' and disappear out of their lives when a bigger, better job prospect presented itself.

She didn't think she could bear the heartache. Trust was a much more precious commodity than she'd ever given it credit for.

'An MRI room can be made ready...' Leon's eyes dipped to his tablet '...now.'

Lizzy forced herself to regroup. 'Right. Good.

Are you up for walking today, Gabrielle? Or are you happier in a wheelchair?'

Once they'd set Gabrielle up in the MRI scanner, and Matteo's foot-rub had been rejected in favour of a trip down to the local *piazza*, to see if he could find any healthy snacks, Leon and Lizzy went to the imaging room, overseeing the scan.

After a few minutes of silently staring at the images appearing on the screen, Lizzy turned to Leon. 'I'm sorry.'

'For what?'

'Behaving like a loon.' She pointed her index fingers at her stomach. 'It might be the cowardly option, but I'm holding someone else responsible for my behaviour.'

'Well, in that case, apology accepted.' Leon pressed a hand to his chest and then, as if an idea had just struck him, held up a finger. 'On one condition.'

'What's that?' She grinned warily.

'Let me take you on a tour of Rome. Today.'

Oh! Well, that was loads better than baring all her deepest darkest fears. Even so…it was time away from the hospital—and, more dangerously, time *with Leon*.

'We've already seen the Trevi Fountain.'

He huffed out a supercilious laugh. *'Cara!'* He shook his head in mock sorrow. 'You think that's Rome?'

He reached out and tucked a wayward curl behind her ear, his fingers brushing the soft down of her cheek as he did so. *Goosebumps.*

'There is so much more to Rome than the Trevi Fountain.'

She looked at her patient, at the scans appearing on the screen of the babies she'd been tasked to deliver healthy and well. She was well known for her ability to pore over image after image for hours on end, but it would be a shame to fly all this way and not see even a few of the wonders of Rome. Beyond the gelato, of course.

Another image flashed onto the screen.

Her nerve-endings leapt to attention.

There. The left ventricle valve.

She squinted at the image, her brain whirring away, imagining herself placing a stent into the valve. It was going to be a tricky surgery, but achievable.

'Deal accepted. On one of *my* conditions.'

'Okay…?' Leon nodded for her to go ahead.

Her conciliatory expression morphed into the

type of grin a child might wear when it was about to be presented with an ice cream sundae.

'Remember when you talked about the 3D lab?'

He nodded again.

'Can we print 3D versions of the babies now and at each week until thirty-two weeks? In utero. Obvs.'

'Assolutatmente.' His smile matched hers at the idea. 'We can get everyone in…do a few practice rounds of the surgery.' His eyes narrowed. 'On one more condition.'

She frowned and feigned a grumpy huff. 'What? An afternoon out and about in Rome isn't enough for you?'

'No,' he said. 'As a matter of fact, it isn't. I want you to come back and stay at my apartment from now on. Unless there is a genuine emergency.'

Her instinct was to protest. She stopped herself. It was becoming a bad habit, and one she would have to break if Leon really meant what he'd said about wanting to be involved in her and their baby's lives.

She closed her eyes and gave them a rub. From this moment on, she vowed, she would look at Leon through clear, unbiased, non-judgmental eyes. The past was the past and the future was a brand-new thing.

And God help her if he didn't look even more gorgeous when she opened them again.

CHAPTER TEN

LIZZY REACHED OUT and grabbed Leon's hand. 'I can't see!'

'You can.' He put his free hand to the small of her back and guided her to the centre of the glass flooring that was at the heart of the ancient, subterranean *palazzo*. 'Look—see the lights there?'

Lizzy drew in a quick breath. 'Are those…?'

'Public baths,' Leon said, his voice low to match the magical surroundings. 'Second century AD, they think. They would've been adjacent to what is now the *palazzo*.'

'And these other rooms, the tiles, the kitchen areas—those are all centuries old?'

'Around five hundred years,' he confirmed. 'The *palazzo* went through numerous renovations, of course, and as you can see…' he gestured to the walls soaring above them '…so has the rest of Rome.'

Lizzy shook her head in disbelief, leaning into

Leon's hand, a movement that seemed so natural anyone around them would assume they were a couple. A movement that elicited a hundred questions for Leon, who knew they weren't.

'I can't believe we're *seven metres* below the rest of Rome!'

He laughed appreciatively. 'I couldn't either, when I first saw it. These elements of the *palazzo* were only discovered recently—and excavated this century—and the addition of the glass floors, so people can walk freely above the remains, is even more recent.'

'Palazzo Valentini...' Lizzy sighed. 'It sounds so romantic, doesn't it?'

Leon gave her hand a squeeze, and to his surprise received a small squeeze of acknowledgment in return. Tipping his head to give the top of her head a kiss, just as he would have five years ago, seemed the natural thing to do—so he did it. She leant into him again, then shot him a shy smile.

Perhaps it was being cloaked in the low lighting. Perhaps it was holding hands. Perhaps it was simply being with Lizzy. But standing amidst the remains of an ancient family's household, where lives had been lived and lost, filled him with a profound sense of longing.

What sort of history would the two of them leave behind? And, more to the point, what sort of future would they have?

He felt as if someone had taken the well-worn and very familiar carpet he'd been walking on his entire life, yanked it out from underneath him and—just like in this *palazzo*—uncovered metres and metres of memories and emotions to excavate.

Could he do that? Clear away the anger and the pain from his past to allow for a bright, loving future with Lizzy?

'And how was it you got us tickets?' Lizzy asked. 'The couple behind us in the queue said they'd had to book months ago.'

'A patient.'

She nodded. She'd clearly had a few of those as well. Patients who were so grateful they promised any favour at any time as thanks for bringing their child into the world.

They continued walking past the archaeological finds—ancient pots women had filled with water, tiled benches men would have relaxed on, no doubt professing to be 'thinking great thoughts', and of course bedrooms.

A thought struck him as they entered another pitch-black room, the glass floor their only support as they gazed on the archaeological finds a good three metres below them, lit by dim flood-lights. Believing that love was enough to sustain a relationship was a bit like stepping onto one of these invisible floors.

Ahead of him he saw a young child drop to his knees and crawl along it, finding safety in proximity to the floor that supported him. Was that what he'd been doing? Clinging to a false support—to his belief that being alone meant less heartache—when in actual fact sometimes enduring the heartache made moments like this that much more rewarding.

His gut instinct when Lizzy had told him about their child had been to ask her to marry him. He had to trust that. Even if it did seem insane. Walking on the moon had seemed impossible at one juncture. As had painting the extraordinary arches and domes of the Sistine Chapel. But people who'd believed in the impossible had done it.

The magical atmosphere of the *palazzo* suddenly turned claustrophobic. Enough museums. Enough of the past. It was time to build his own future. One that included the gorgeous blonde by his side. One that made them a family.

He leant down and whispered into Lizzy's ear. 'Let's get some gelato.'

Lizzy looked up at him, her lips quirked into a smile, but her brows were furrowed together and she looked perplexed. 'Now?'

'Yes. Now.'

'We've not had supper yet.'

'Bah.' He waved away the feeble protest. 'It's only five o'clock. A perfect time for gelato and then…' An idea struck. He dropped her a wink. 'C'mon. Follow me. I know just the way to build up an appetite.'

Lizzy's heart pounded in her chest as she stumbled blindly alongside Leon as he led her through the darkened corridors of the subterranean *palazzo*.

Sex.

He was talking about sex, wasn't he?

What other way was there to build up an appetite for supper?

She raced back over the conversations they'd had which had led up to her agreeing to take this tour of Rome and wondered if there had been anything in her behaviour that had screamed, *Have your wicked way with me, you sexy Italian beast, you!*

Hmm…

There was nothing obvious…

But they were holding hands.

Was that a new signal that a lovemaking session was on the horizon?

Oh, God. She was so out of touch with how things worked. With her and Leon back in the day, things had been extraordinarily simple. Work. Sex. Sleep. Repeat. A spectacular combination of energies that had somehow morphed into her convincing herself she was madly in love with him. Something she was meant to have doused last New Year's Eve, when she'd left a sleeping Leon alone in his honeymoon suite.

Leon silently led her out of the *palazzo*, his hand holding hers, his thumb distractedly… or tactically…rubbing the back of her hand as thoughts of unbuttoning his shirt and whipping his belt out of the loops of his hip-hugging trousers stirred her nervous system into a frenzy.

By the time they'd bought the obligatory postcards, left the building and blinked and adjusted their eyes to the bright late-afternoon sunshine, Lizzy was so close to pouncing on Leon it was ridiculous. How could one solitary man smell like a pastry shop and the citrus aisle of a supermarket all at once?

So many questions to which there were no answers...

Which was why she adopted a casually uninterested air as she leant against a pile of rocks that had no doubt been part of a palace three thousand years ago, stared at Leon, and then huskily asked, 'So...what's this big plan of yours?'

'Voilà!'

Leon stepped to one side and threw out his arm, pointing towards an electric bicycle rental company.

Oh.

Her spirits deflated more than they should. She'd been quite keen on the idea of sanctioned sex.

'Yay!' She waved a pair of invisible pompoms. 'A bike-ride!'

'Electric bikes,' he corrected. 'I've always wanted to do this.'

'Really?' Weird... He lived here, and this was a very touristy thing to do.

'Si!' He gave one of those nonchalant shrugs of his. 'I grew up here, but I never really saw things fresh, you know? The Colosseum, the

Parthenon, the *palazzo* we just went to. They were all just buildings I used as signposts rather than things I really looked at.'

She nodded, seeing his point. Sydney was the same for her. She'd only ever been to the Opéra House on a school trip, and more recently on a blind date she'd had to abort before they'd even got to their seats because she'd been called to surgery. She'd never taken a harbour cruise, never seen an open-air film in the Botanical Gardens, never been up the Sydney Tower Eye…

Crikey. Was work the only thing she'd done since she'd returned from her internship? It was looking that way.

'This isn't some clever way to show off your glutes, is it?'

A girl could dream.

He snorted. 'I thought it'd be a nice way to build up an appetite. Unless you think it's too hot?'

Oh, she was hungry all right. But not for carbs.

She pursed her lips. 'You call this hot? Come to Australia, mate. I'll show you hot.'

The late spring air thickened between them. The sexual electricity she'd felt surging out of her was now zinging both ways.

Leon's dark eyes locked with hers. 'Would you like that? If I came to Australia?'

It wasn't a flippant question. It was a genuine one.

And it felt as intimate as if she were lying unclothed, waiting for his touch.

Did she want that? For him to see the little cocoon of work and home life she'd created for herself?

It was pretty embarrassing, actually. All her friends were from work. Since her mother had passed away she pretty much only saw her dad when she had to. Birthdays. Christmas. If she wasn't working. She didn't have any hobbies or social clubs to take Leon to. No surfing skills to show off nor masses of friends to introduce him to at a regularly scheduled champagne brunch.

In all honesty her life in Sydney wasn't that different from the little cocoon Leon had made for himself here. A bells-and-whistles workplace that demanded attention at all hours, most days of the week. A home literally a jog away from said hospital. The only difference in their lifestyles was that her place was near the beach and had more Crayon drawings.

'Sure. One day. So…' She rubbed her hands together enthusiastically. 'Right, then! Let's get exploring.'

Two hours later they pulled their bicycles back into the hire station, smiles tugging their lips from ear to ear. Leon had been right. Seeing Rome through Lizzy's eyes had made his home town about a thousand times better.

She had a keen eye for finding small pieces of art tucked into doorframes and olive trees defying their cement surroundings and producing tiny little olives, just waiting for the summer sun to ripen them.

They'd stopped in the centre of Rome's oldest bridge, thought to have been built in 62BC, and marvelled at all the people and their outfits and the modes of transport it must have borne witness to.

They'd walked their cycles through the Jewish Quarter—one of the world's oldest ghettos.

They'd stood in silence, their hands brushing each other's, in the centre of a two-thousand-year-old church so ripe with atmosphere in the form of incense and candlelight that they'd both, in tandem, turned to light candles, neither one asking who they were lighting them for, but each knowing instinctively the solitary flames they lit were for someone close to them. Someone for whom they wished peace. Their mothers.

An unspoken peace had settled between the pair of them as they'd glided through the thinning crowds. People rushing home or, as was the case with most tourists, couples wandering hand in hand, paying attention to anything and nothing, happy to be sharing this glorious city with someone they loved.

And Leon was one of them.

'That was great fun. Thank you.'

Lizzy went up on tiptoe to give Leon's cheek a kiss, but their helmets knocked together and she lurched backwards.

He grabbed hold of her waist and steadied her. Unbuckling her helmet, he slid it off her head, enjoying watching her hair as it tumbled out of the helmet and over her shoulders. He took his own off then, because nothing else seemed to be the right thing to do, and he kissed her properly.

It was the kind of kiss he'd been aching to give her since she'd arrived here in Rome but had been too afraid to lest it meant committing to something he wouldn't be able to make good on. Sure, he'd proposed. Lizzy had called him on it. But there had been a hell of a lot of water under the proverbial bridge in such a short time. They were sharing lives, a child, and the world they saw through separate lenses was being melded into one beautiful kaleidoscope of shared history...

It seemed like something he could do. And the only way to find out if they could be together was to be open and honest. And...like on those glass floors...he wouldn't know until he took the first step.

When they finally separated, Lizzy's cheeks were pink. 'You were right,' she said.

'About what?'

'I needed that before supper.'

He laughed, not asking for clarification as to whether she meant the cycle ride or the kiss.

'Want to eat Chez Cassanetti or out?'

She considered the options for a moment and then said, 'Out.'

He smiled. 'I know just the place.'

'This looks...erm...interesting...'

Leon's eyebrows performed a little *wait and see* jig.

After having walked past several dozen utterly gorgeous, flower bedecked, history-laden *ristorantes* and *trattorias, pescerias* and *tavolas* and, yes, even some rather alluring *pizzerias*, Lizzy had tried to summon a smile when they'd stopped in front of the plain-fronted, no-nonsense *osteria* Leon had chosen—the Italian equivalent of a gastropub, Leon explained, without the chalkboard menus and the aesthetically pleasing *olde-worlde* environment.

She was starving, so frankly a hotdog would do at this juncture, but she was trusting that some insider knowledge had made him pick this plain-tiled, sixties Brutalist street-front eatery called, simply, Osteria Rosso.

She was also completely giddy. Her every nerve-ending was still crackling from that kiss. It had been the type of kiss that swept through her body over and over again in the best possible way. It had coincided with the golden hour—that perfect moment before sunset, when everything was bathed in a peachy-golden hue. So… weirdly…even Brutalist architecture didn't look half bad. Especially as she was holding hands with Leon—the same hand that had occasionally, almost absently, slipped to the small of her back to guide her this way or that as they navigated the ancient streets of central Rome, bringing yet another set of tingles for her body to enjoy.

What on earth any of it meant was another story. But for this moment she was happy to let her hormones enjoy the ride.

There was, surprisingly, a queue. Every now and again a large, rosy-cheeked woman appeared at the door and eyed up whoever was next in line, and then, seemingly randomly, admitted them or turned them away.

On her third such journey she caught Leon's eye. He gave a little wave. She beckoned him in.

After they'd been seated at what might easily be considered the best table—by the window, overlooking a leafy cobbled street—Lizzy asked, 'What favours have you done for her?'

'Grandbaby,' he answered.

Lizzy raised a *tell me more* eyebrow.

'Spina bifida,' he said simply.

'In utero?'

He nodded, his eyes dropping to the handwritten menu they'd been handed, along with a pair of soft drinks and a recommendation to try the fish special. It was, according to the owner, indescribably delicious.

Lizzy stared at Leon for a few moments as he read, absorbing what she'd always known about him but never acknowledged. That rare spinal surgery was a gamechanger. If left until birth, an unclosed spinal column could cause irreversible brain damage and severe trauma-based injuries to the nerves below a baby's waist. Surgery wasn't a cure-all, but it certainly gave the child a better shot at a normal life.

'You don't like to brag on yourself, do you?'

He looked across at her. *'Che?'*

'You don't make a big show of who you are and how unbelievable a surgeon you are.'

His shoulders did a tell-tale lift and drop. 'Why would I? It's about the outcome, isn't it? Not who created it?'

All at once she saw how generous and huge his heart was. He was like the very best chocolates at Christmas. A hard, crisp shell with an utterly gooey core. He didn't do any of his groundbreaking surgeries to raise his stature. He'd all but handed the baton to her when she'd arrived for the Bianchi case. Sure, he was the lead doctor, and he would also overseeing Grace's care while she focused on Hope's HLHS, but beyond that first day, when she'd been stupidly cross because he'd taken the lead at the group lecture, where—*duh!*—she had known about as much as everyone else bar him, he really wasn't a limelight kind of guy.

'Why do you do this?' she asked.

'What? Surgery?'

'Yeah, but...little tiny babies. Babies who don't have personalities yet. Babies who haven't yet breathed oxygen. When you claimed to never want babies for yourself.'

They both stared at each other a bit after that.

Then, 'Why do you do this?' she asked again.

He put down the menu and took a sip of his drink as he considered his answer. It was another trait she hadn't really etched into her portrait of him yet. He was a thinker. He liked to mull things over before committing. Which meant his marriage proposal genuinely had come from the heart. Which meant...*gulp*...that Leon had actually genuinely proposed to her.

'I don't want to be alone when I live!'

'I suppose... I suppose it's changed over the years,' he finally said.

'From what to what?' Lizzy asked straight away.

'From something that seemed impossible—something only extraordinary people could do—to something that is essential, regardless of the merit that comes with it.'

Hmm…that was too esoteric for her. 'Explain,' she demanded.

'I suppose I do it more for the mothers than anyone.'

'How so?' It was a laudable reason, but she really wanted to get underneath the reason *why*.

He traced his finger around the top of his water glass, then looked her in the eye. 'Have I ever told you about my childhood?'

Three times they waved away Concetta, the proprietress, until eventually she gave up and brought them what she thought they should eat.

A common practice in Italy, Leon assured her. For a place where restaurateurs did not believe the customer knew best. *They* did.

Half an hour and one plate of extraordinary *antipasti* later, Lizzy felt as shell-shocked as Leon looked. They were finally having the type of conversation most couples had in those first precious few weeks of courtship. The type of *Who are you, really?* conversation that demanded all the attention that neither Lizzy nor Leon had had the time or energy for, because of their insanely busy surgical schedules and because… Well, because that hadn't been what they *did*.

They'd worked. They'd competed. They'd sparked off one another. They'd made love. But they definitely hadn't talked. Not like this.

They both sat back in their chairs as their *secondis* were delivered. Pasta for Leon and— *oh, yum*—an amazing-looking risotto with fish for Lizzy.

When the waitress had left Lizzy asked, 'Why is this the first time you've told me about it? Your past?'

He twirled his fork through a tumble of *spaghettini* dappled with delicate little clams, glossy from a clear broth. 'Is your food all right?' he asked lightly, as if he hadn't just bared his soul. He poised his fork by his mouth, about to eat the expert swirl of pasta.

'Delicious.' It was—gorgeous grilled seabass with some beautiful tiny fresh peas in a lemony risotto—but she held up a finger. 'Can we go back to the whole thing of your father getting up in the middle of your supper and leaving for ever, please?'

He nodded, his eyes dropping to the bowl of pasta, his fork making half-hearted stabs at the clams swimming in the broth.

'What do you want to know?' he asked.

'Did you ever see him again?'

'Once.'

'So, he came back, then?'

'No. His wife in Scandinavia found out about me and invited me to spend the summer with them.'

'He'd remarried?'

'*Si.*' he confirmed tonelessly. 'Right away. Marriage, children, a holiday cabin on an is-land—the whole nine yards, as they say.'

He looked up, but appeared to be looking through her, as if reliving that summer afresh. His dark eyes took on a haunted hollowness that made Lizzy's heart ache. 'And…?'

He cleared his throat and gave her a tight smile. 'And it turned out he would've preferred it if she hadn't. He didn't like being reminded that he'd made mistakes.'

'He saw you as a mistake?' Lizzy put her fork down, unable to match the delicious meal with the awful story he was telling.

'He saw being with my mother as a mistake, and therefore anything that had been affiliated with her—like me—was also a mistake.'

And then it became crystal-clear to her. He was helping all those pregnant mothers have as perfect a baby as possible. He was preventing 'mistakes'.

Her voice caught in her throat as she reached out to him. 'I'm so sorry, Leon.'

'Don't be.' He accepted her touch but soon pulled away to take a drink of water. 'I'm not telling you for your pity.' His eyes flared, then steadied. 'I'm telling you because I want you to understand why I've behaved the way I have. Why I held you at arm's length before we'd had a chance to see where things could go.'

She sat on this information for a minute. She'd been a willing participant in their *when the internships are done, we're done* thing, but if he'd heard her say she loved him...if he'd said he loved her too...would they be together now? Have children already? Be a family.

He toyed with his food for a minute, then abruptly his face tightened with unwelcome emotion. 'My father's wife had a stillborn baby when I was there. They sent me back straight away. She never said anything—she never would have—but my father did.'

'What on earth did he say?' Lizzy asked, though her churning gut was already telling her the awful answer to her question.

'He blamed me. Said my appearance had caused too much stress and strain and that I'd caused the baby's death.'

Lizzy's hands flew to her chest. 'I'm so, *so* sorry, Leon.'

She didn't bother telling him it wasn't true. He knew that. But knowing about the incident threw another swathe of light on Leon's complicated past. He didn't explain further, but he didn't have to. He had become an antenatal surgeon because he wanted to fix what he hadn't been able to fix as a child.

Her heart absolutely ached for him.

All the pieces of the *Why does Leon behave the way he does?* puzzle were in place now.

A boy who was abandoned by his father through no fault of his own.

A mother who withdrew her affections because of a broken heart that had swiftly turned bitter.

An adolescence spent being told to retreat from happiness because it only led to pain and, heartbreakingly, seeing the evidence to back it up.

No wonder he hadn't ever had faith in something as ethereal as love. His life had been mired in rejection and blame.

'Did you tell your mother?' Lizzy asked eventually. 'About what had happened?'

He shook his head. 'No point.'

'But she could have at least consoled you,' Lizzy shot back, knowing even as she spoke that the mother Leon had described would have defined love as a mirage designed to fool a person into giving their very best to another, only to be abandoned and left heartbroken and alone.

'Did you light your candle for her?' Lizzy asked, again already knowing the answer.

He nodded. 'And you?'

'My mum.' She left it at that, hoping they could leave putting the microscope to her own less than happy childhood for another day.

Leon tilted his head so that he could catch her eyes with his, those dark, beautifully familiar eyes of his searching hers for a cue as to whether or not she wanted to talk.

She dropped her gaze to his plate.

'Want some?' he asked.

She nodded, suddenly strangely ravenous.

He dipped his fork into the centre of the dish and created a gorgeous whorl of pasta and clams, then lifted the forkful, dripping, up to her mouth.

As she took a bite she looked up and met his eyes. What she saw made her heart skip a beat. She saw longing. The same longing she tried to hide from the world. A bone-deep ache to be part of a couple. So she would never have to worry about being loved. So she would never have to think about who she could turn to when she was happy, sad, tired, anxious or over the moon. Part of a couple with a partner in life who felt exactly the same way. Two people who were each other's homing beacons, providing a place of safety and security in a world where so many things were beyond their control. Two people who could raise a child together...

'Should we try it out?' she asked, after finishing the mouthful of succulent pasta.

'What?' He shook his head, not understanding.

'Us. Being a couple. While we're here.'

'What? You mean you're accepting my proposal?' His eyes went wide.

She wasn't going to go that far, but... 'How about we consider this a new beginning?'

He looked at her intently. He was listening. And looking damn hot. Which was distracting.

'Explain,' he said.

'We just...see how we go. Try being a couple.'

'In the same flat?' Leon asked, well aware that she hadn't exactly agreed to move back into his flat with him.

'Yes,' she said, her heart skipping a beat as

she did so. 'In the same flat, in the same hospital, working on the same case. It's like an intensive cramming for a final exam.'

He laughed at that. 'What? You want to look at this as "cramming", to see if we'd be any good at marriage?'

She shook her head and gave him what she hoped was a cheeky grin. 'We're cramming so we can see if we'll be good together—warts and all. Because…babies mean warts.'

His expression sobered, the reality of their impending parenthood clearly taking a hold of him, and then that hard-won smile of his lit up his face as he took her hand in his and said simply, 'Our baby won't have warts.'

She laughed. 'You know I don't mean it literally. I just mean…this is scary. For both of us. Neither of us has any experience at being in a relationship—a proper one, that has peaks and troughs and mistakes and forgiveness.'

'You mean one that lasts a lifetime?'

His words landed in her heart with an explosion of heat. Yes. That was exactly what she meant. And it scared the living daylights out of her.

'I mean a happy, honest, *respectful* one,' she qualified, thinking of her parents' marriage, which had lasted her mother's lifetime, but certainly hadn't been a happy one. Nor respectful. 'We're heading into the wilderness here, you and I.'

'What do you mean?'

'Neither of us has really had the best of examples, have we?'

He shook his head, giving her the space to continue if she wanted to talk about her own childhood. But she didn't, and by then Concetta had cleared their dinner plates and brought two ridiculously beautiful servings of pannacotta, and it seemed a perfect time to let the intensity of their conversation have some room to breathe.

She lifted up the tiny glass of herbal digestif their hostess had slipped onto the table next to her dessert bowl. 'To seeing how we go?'

Leon lifted his own glass and shared a smile with her—one that actually looked as excited as she felt. 'To seeing how we go.'

CHAPTER ELEVEN

LEON HAD NEVER believed holding hands could deliver such promise. And yet here he was, walking through the streets of Rome, holding hands with the woman carrying his child, hoping he had the strength to make good on the commitment they'd just made to one another.

As commitments went it was fairly vague.

Let's see how it goes.

Not exactly *Till death us do part*, but it was a start. Not bad for two commitment-shy, work-obsessed control freaks like the two of them.

Abruptly he pulled her into a doorway, cupped her face with his hands and kissed her until they both lost their breath.

'What was that for?' she asked, her cheeks pinkened with, very possibly, a hint of shyness. This was, after all, the first time ever they had knowingly gone home together as a bona fide couple since New York. It felt like being a teenager. It felt like falling in love.

'Because,' he said, dropping a kiss on her nose.

Because he loved her, and he didn't know if his version of love was enough.

He pushed his fears to the side, reminding himself that they were taking this risk together. He wasn't alone. He had by his side the one woman he could trust to give him the room to make mistakes.

He slid his arm over her shoulders as they headed towards home. This felt nice. It felt good! It felt *right*…the *Let's see how it goes* approach.

When they reached his flat and got into the geriatric lift, the sexual tension that had been building between them on their walk home escalated.

Lizzy teasingly traced her finger from the base of his throat down to his belt buckle, and then suddenly, with a she-devil smile, tugged him in close.

Something deep and primal surged to the fore and spread like wildfire through his bloodstream. For the first time ever, he didn't care if it took a lifetime for the lift to inch its way up to the top floor. It gave him time to run the backs of his fingers along Lizzy's sides. To feel her arch into him as his fingertips lightly grazed the edges of her neck, her breasts, her waist…

His hands shifted to caress her thighs— which, to his satisfaction, elicited a soft moan. Without a second thought he lifted her up so that she was straddling his waist, kissing her as if his life depended upon it. And in this moment, it felt as if it did.

The moment the lift juddered into place on the seventh floor he yanked open the iron gate and, still carrying and kissing Lizzy, unlocked his door and took her, without any consultation, to his bedroom.

She didn't raise a solitary objection.

He sat down on the bed with Lizzy straddling him, her fingers already busy undoing his shirt buttons. In one swift, fluid move, he gathered the hem of her dress in his hands and pulled it up and over her head, relishing the sight of her body. Her breasts were fuller. Her curves softer. Everything about her was beautiful.

He shifted her gently to the bed, laying her down so that he could, for the first time, properly admire the soft curve of her belly. Their child was growing in there. Their beautiful, perfect child.

He dropped kiss after kiss upon her stomach as Lizzy ran her fingers through his hair—softly at first, and then, as the kisses descended, dropping her nails to his shoulders and scraping them against his skin as she groaned, 'I want you inside me.'

With each featherlight touch, kiss and caress, Lizzy felt as though her body was being lit from within—as if light was radiating like sunshine from a place she could only define as her very essence. It felt like being lit up by fireworks and enormous fistfuls of glitter.

They explored each other's body with a luxuriousness that didn't acknowledge time or space or the need for sleep or air. They were one another's oxygen. They were one another's life force. And Lizzy had never felt more alive in her life.

Leon lifted himself and then wholly, completely entered her, his eyes connecting with hers in an electricity she'd never known before—a shared energy that could only mean that for the first time neither of them was holding back.

She cried out in pleasure as he began to move with the rhythm of her hips. Arcing, pushing, savouring each moment as if it were a precious memory. There was a complexity to their love-making that was new. A feverish need to be as close together as humanly possible that went beyond those early lust-fuelled days in New York. What they needed now was different. Went deeper. Demanded more.

And that, Lizzy realised as she tipped her head back and Leon dropped kiss after heated kiss along her throat, was the key, wasn't it? Knowing one another's foibles. Knowing one another's pain. Hopes, dreams, desires, fears… All of it.

A sliver of her acknowledged that she'd not been nearly as open with Leon as he had with her, but she'd get there—now that they were taking on their fears…and hopes…together.

'Is this all right?' Leon asked as once again he eased his erection deeper into her, his hands pressing into the bed, his arm muscles growing taut as, with each movement, he turned her insides into liquid heat with stroke after stroke.

'More than,' she managed. And she meant it.

She'd thought the lovemaking they'd shared on New Year's Eve had been other-worldly, but she'd been wrong. That had been fuelled by…

not revenge, exactly, but it certainly hadn't been by love.

This shared synchronicity they were experiencing now—the vulnerability of it—*this* was what making love actually was. Sharing the most intimate thing a couple could, knowing they might fail at being together and trying anyway.

Each time their stomachs touched, their thighs connected or, more urgently, she felt him withdraw completely and then tease at the junction of her thighs, she fought the urge to wrap her legs around him and tug him to her, so their bodies would reach that inevitable moment when they organically moved as one, urgently, uncontrollably, to reach the climax she was so desperately close to.

But she didn't. She forced herself to slow to the achingly luxurious cadence Leon had set, drawing out the pleasure as long as possible, trusting him, knowing that she could have faith in him to bring her to climax with him. Just as she had to have faith that he could change and that she too could change, she quietly acknowledged.

Life was complicated. Just like in the surgical ward, life was full of ups and downs, and, if there was anyone in the world she thought she could take that roller coaster ride with, it was Leon. The father of her child.

Their eyes caught and cinched.

She knew what they were communicating to one another.

Now.

By silent agreement, the intensity of Leon's movements gathered pace. Her hips met him thrust for thrust, her breath quickening, and soon enough her body was no longer having to obey her commands but merely following its natural rhythms, so that before her brain had a chance to catch up the two of them were pressed together so completely she felt as though Leon's body were directly communicating with her. His heartbeat matched hers. His racing blood ran in sync with hers. Their orgasms matched each other's with such force it doubled the pleasure and the intensity.

When, later, they were lying side by side, their breaths steadying, and as the long day began to take hold of them, she let herself focus on individual sensations. Leon's hand on her hip. His long, dark eyelashes. The hair on his leg brushing her smooth one. His scent, warm and citrusy, magnified into something like a warm summer afternoon in an orchard by his body's heat. Their eyes…his dark ones, her light ones… gazing sleepily into each other's.

She almost told him how she felt. That she loved him. But then a light fluttering in her stomach erased everything else from her mind. Her practical side told her it was far too soon to be feeling anything close to kicks or movements. That for a first-time mother such as herself, it was normal not to feel anything until twenty weeks. But…

'What? Did you feel it? Did you feel the baby?'

She grinned. Leon was clearly throwing his training to the winds, too.

'I don't think so—not really. But…' She moved his hand to her belly. 'Perhaps I sensed it? It's a bit of a learning curve, all this mother's intuition, isn't it?'

He shrugged. 'You're going to be the expert on that one. I suppose I'll be learning what it feels like to be an anxious father, unable to do anything apart from…' He pushed his full lips out as he thought of something a pregnant woman might want. 'I could peel some grapes for you?'

She laughed and rolled her eyes. 'No! I think,

as we're in Rome, you being a gelato angel would probably do the trick. And salami. The peppery kind. With fennel.'

'A gelato angel, eh?' he said, his accent thickening as his voice lowered. 'Is that what you're going to make our child out of? Gelato and fennel salami?'

'Yes,' she quipped, feeling strangely happy that her baby was going to grow fuelled by the beautiful foods available in this equally beautiful city, occasionally fed to her, as today's perfect forkful of pasta had been, by the world's most beautiful man.

He gently eased her onto her back so he could spread his hand across her belly, dropping the odd kiss exactly where their baby was growing. One of the advantages, she thought, of having created a child with an antenatal surgeon. The disadvantages, of course, being that they both knew the countless things that could go wrong.

The moment was so perfect, though, that she pushed all that knowledge to the side and enjoyed feeling Leon's hand on her stomach, his lips whispering against her tummy as he…

'What are you doing?'

'I'm teaching our *piccolo pompelmo* Italian.

It'll be an advantage in life. To enter the world bilingual, *si*?'

'You know it can't hear. A couple more weeks yet.'

He waved away the fact. 'Our baby is more advanced than other babies. Look at its parents!' He struck a Brainiac pose that, being done naked, made him look a lot like Michelangelo's *David*.

She giggled as his lips brushed against her tummy while he murmured words she was pretty certain were all food-based. 'Are you telling the baby what foods to ask for?'

'Maybe…' Leon threw her a cheeky grin. 'We don't want it being raised on sub-standard cuisine. Not when it has the best Rome has to offer, right?'

'Hang on a minute! My country has amazing food, too.' She shot him a mischievous look. 'If you don't watch it, I'm going to find an Aussie deli and feed it exclusively on Lamingtons and meat pies.'

Leon made a tsking noise and instantly began speaking to the tiny baby inside her in characteristically impassioned Italian. She fought the instinct to combatively counter with a list of the genuinely delicious foods Australia had to offer.

This wasn't a contest and Leon wasn't her father. He wasn't trying to dominate her, or box her into a way of living that suffocated the woman she really was. He was a proud father-to-be wanting his child to delight in the things he delighted in. To enjoy the things that brought him joy—or the things that, perhaps more realistically, he'd never been allowed to enjoy. Not with his family anyway.

This was his chance every bit as much as it was hers to give a child the life each of them had ached for. Happy, carefree, and full of love. She would have to learn to allow Leon the freedom to love their child in his way as much as she wanted to love the child in hers, the most important point being that they both wanted their child to feel loved.

Lizzy drew her fingers through Leon's silky hair, eventually dissolving into giggles as his lips brushed against her tummy with a never-ending menu. *Bucatini amatriciana, tonnarelli cacio e pepe, suppli, carciofi de fritte.* And the list went on and on.

She leant back against the pillow, little trills of excitement running through her each time Leon said *'mamma'* or *'papà'*.

The enormity of it hit her afresh. She was

going to be a mother. Leon was going to be a father. The baby they would have was right here in her belly, growing, developing, just days away from being able to distinguish between its father's voice and its mother's laugh. She prayed those would be the sounds their child would hear throughout his or her life. Sounds of joy. Love. Happiness. She herself had no idea what it was like to grow up in a happy household.

'Let's find out,' she said abruptly.

'What?' Leon looked up, confused. 'You want to know what the special is at Osteria Russo to-morrow?'

'No,' she said, with an urgency she hadn't re-alised she'd been building up to. 'I want to know if it's a boy or girl. I want to call it something other than *pompelmo*.'

He looked at her, his eyes communicating all the things words simply didn't have the capac-ity to embrace, and nodded. 'As you wish.'

CHAPTER TWELVE

'READY?' LEON ASKED.

'As I'll ever be.' She gave him a nod. 'Go on. Do it.'

He laughed, considering the fact that she'd been saying she was ready for the past two weeks and then, just as he was about to put the sonography wand on her stomach, always changed her mind.

This sort of surprise, she'd told him as she batted away his hand, only came once. They didn't want to misread the scan, which might easily happen if they did it too early.

He'd nodded, bitten his cheek, and kept back all the things he could have said—like, *We do this for a living*, or *Who cares what sex it is so long as it's healthy?* or, more daringly, *We could always have another child after this one. Be a proper big, bustling family.* The type he'd always wanted to be a part of but never once admitted—not even to himself.

They'd reached a point where they were going to have to tell someone about the baby—Giovanni being the obvious candidate—but the more aware he was of the child growing inside Lizzy, the more her stomach arced and swelled, the more Leon wanted to stay inside the little private bubble the two of them had been living in since that magical night they'd made love.

There, had, of course, been other nights, other moments of intimacy, but that night had marked a turning point. A sea change in his approach to the life he wanted to live and who he wanted to live it with.

They'd agreed to keep things professional at the hospital, not wanting to fuel the permanent hunger for gossip, but life had a way of forcing people's hands and they were no different. This morning, when Lizzy hadn't been able to fit into any of the clothes she'd packed, they had known that the truth, if not already out there, would have to become common knowledge. Which was why they'd decided to find out the sex of their baby today—before Lizzy's pregnancy was made public.

'Okay…' He held the wand above her belly. 'Are you ready to see the cucumber?'

She smirked at him. 'I thought we'd gone with *pompelmo*?'

He shrugged that easy shrug of his. 'You say *pompelmo*. I say *cetriolo*.' And then he put the wand on her belly.

They watched in silence as the screen flickered to life, their child's heartbeat almost instantly filling the room with that gorgeous *whoosh-whoosh* signifying life.

'He's got fingerprints now.'

'Or she,' Lizzy corrected softly, knowing from the way the baby was positioned that they couldn't yet know.

'Look at those little feet!'

Leon whispered something she couldn't quite catch in Italian, but it sounded like a prayer of gratitude. Then they watched as he moved the wand here and there, one of them occasionally saying a word like *ears* or *toes* or *perfect*.

'Do you see?'

Leon had finally hit the sweet spot in the scan.

Lizzy's face lit up. 'I do.'

'We're going to have a little girl.'

Her brows dived together. 'You're happy with that, right?'

'I'd be happy if you had a koala!'

She laughed, then made a dismissive noise. 'Don't be ridiculous. You look nothing like a koala.'

'Oh?' He put his head between her and the sonography screen. 'What *do* I look like, then?'

Her smile softened as her cheeks lightly pinkened. 'Like no one else in the world.'

'And that's a good thing?' he asked.

'That's the very best thing,' she replied, reaching out to press the kiss she'd put on her fingertips to his lips. 'The very best thing of all.'

It should have been a perfect moment. A moment when he told her, once and for all, that he loved her. A moment when he produced a diamond ring from his pocket. A moment when he got down on his knee and asked her to make him the happiest man on earth by agreeing to be part of a family with him and their daughter.

But something about the look in her eyes—the hope, the expectation she had, that things wouldn't come to a natural end as they had back in New York—shifted something inside him that unleashed a sharp, painful rush of age-old fears.

Would he be enough? Could he really stay the

course? Was he the best man for Lizzy to raise a child with? And, more to the point, would loving Lizzy expose him to the heartache his mother had been subjected to when his father had decided he'd rather go leave and pretend none of his marriage had ever happened?

Mercifully, his beeper went off. He didn't want her to see this. To witness the uncertainty in his eyes when he knew what she needed more than anything was a confident, solid, committed man by her side.

Somehow, some way, he told himself as he strode through the hospital corridors towards the surgical ward, where he would help another mother and her child surmount their own difficulties, he hoped he would find a way to hurdle his own.

Lizzy withdrew the laparoscope and discarded the instrument on a tray with a clatter of frustration. The nurse who was helping looked at her, startled. Lizzy wasn't normally a clatterer. Or one to use blue language, for that matter.

'*Scusi,* I—'

Lizzy shook her head and tried to find the words to explain how it was that she'd let emotions get the better of her, but those same emotions seemed to have absorbed her vocabulary. *Urgh.*

She tugged off the surgical cap she'd put on to try and get herself in the zone, but even that hadn't worked. She simply wasn't in the mood. And she'd just killed Hope. And by proxy Grace. Pretend 3D-printed Hope and Grace, but still… She'd killed them.

There was no chance she would be wheeling Gabrielle into the operating theatre when she was feeling like this. Emotional. Distracted. Wondering why the hell Leon had abruptly left her in the middle of finding out they were having a little girl.

Sure, he'd been paged, but she'd seen something happen. Something that had turned his eyes a dangerous shade of dark that had absorbed the warm chocolatey depths she loved.

A pretty dark-haired woman with a lovely Scottish burr walked into the lab. Autumn Fraser. She was the surgeon Giovanni had recruited to head Team Grace once the babies had been safely delivered.

If they got that far, Lizzy thought darkly, glaring at the biocompatible model of the twins.

She grimaced, then forced on a smile. 'G'day. You all right?'

'Hi! Sorry. I was just hoping for a bit of…just trying to find somewhere—' Autumn stopped and started a couple more times until finally settling on, 'I didn't realise anyone else was in here.'

Lizzy instantly saw a kindred spirit. Someone hoping for a quiet space to mull over some extra-complicated thoughts. Her smile instantly grew warm with empathy. She'd had a nice impression of Autumn the smattering of times they'd crossed paths. Obviously they saw each other every day for the briefings, but somehow, apart from a short exchange in the locker room, when they'd promised to have a coffee together and talk about the joys of working with Italian surgeons, they hadn't yet got to know each other.

'Is it okay if I watch?' Autumn asked.

Lizzy stood back from the 'operating table' and held up her hands. 'Too late.'

'Oh?'

'I just killed your patient.'

'Ah…' Autumn stayed near the doorway, taking a quick read of the atmosphere in the room. Her concise nod and step back were an acknowledgement that she understood when a surgeon had had a bad day.

The nurse, whom Lizzy knew had live babies to look after, threw her a glance.

'Grazie mille,' she told her. 'Thank you for helping me work the mistakes out of my system.'

She threw in a laugh and a weird little victory punch, trying to prove she wasn't having an actual, proper meltdown in advance of the quickly approaching real-life surgery.

Autumn let the nurse pass, then hesitated, clearly unsure if she should go in or not.

'It's okay. Come on in, Autumn.'

Staying in a huff wasn't going to make this operation any easier. Also, if she was going to be performing surgery that would ultimately affect Grace's well-being, Autumn needed to be as up to speed as she was.

'Want to help me try again?'

'Delighted to.' Autumn's demeanour changed from wary to proactive. 'I want to get my head wrapped round as many angles of the twins' situation as possible.'

'Smart,' Lizzy said, moving the model she'd just used to one side and pulling another one into its place.

At least the technology was reliable here at St Nicolino's, she thought grumpily. Generous, even. Unlike the humans. The *men* in particular. Well… Not all men. Just the ones called Leon Cassanetti.

He'd been called away hours ago and hadn't bothered to come and find her again. Under normal circumstances she wouldn't have thought twice about it. She wasn't his keeper. But he'd been weird. Very weird…

Her mind raced back to the exam room for the nine hundredth time. What on earth had *happened* in there? They'd been so happy, sharing the joy of discovering they were going to have a daughter, and then, all of a sudden—*kablam!* His smile had disappeared as if someone had ripped his fuse out. Then off he'd gone with an excuse she'd used on at least a dozen dates she hadn't wanted to be on: surgery.

Sure, his excuse was legitimate, seeing as he was at work and a surreptitious walk-by of the surgical board did, in fact, have a list of surgeries Leon would be performing today, but a week ago he would've invited her to come along, or at least they would have had a private little kissing session in one of the on-call rooms in between. But this time….

Whatever. *Jerk.* The big chestnut-haired, espresso-eyed Italian so-and-so could take his 'marry me' to someone less gullible. She had known this would happen. Had known it from the start. The moment she'd agreed to fly over here, in fact.

Yes, she'd known in her heart of hearts that she'd be raising their child on her own—had embraced the fact, even. And then, just as he had back in New York, he'd spun her round that surgically perfect little finger of his and allowed her to believe things might turn out differently.

More fool her.

So it was back to Plan A. Because Plan B, which had always been half-formed at best, was quite clearly not destined for success.

Lizzy talked Autumn through the surgery—which, unsurprisingly, followed an exacting protocol. On the day, of course, there'd be a huge team of medical professionals. Perinatologists, cardiologists, radiologists, foetal surgeons, anaesthetists and, of course, Leon. Today, simply put, she needed to laparoscopically balloon dilate Hope's left heart valve in order to insert a small stent.

They began to work. Autumn asked the occasional question and Lizzy talked her through each move, occasionally lapsing into silence as she slipped first the laparoscope, then the tiny surgical tools, and finally the camera into place.

'And Leon will be monitoring Grace, through-out?'

Lizzy shot Autumn a sharp look. Why did she want to know about Leon? She sternly re-minded herself that any normal surgeon work-ing on a conjoined twins' case would want to know what was happening to 'her' baby during life-altering surgery to the other baby. It was a perfectly innocent and fairly essential question.

'Yes. He'll be there the whole time.'

Maybe Leon had wanted a boy. Could be as simple as that. He just needed time to rebuild the scenarios he'd built for himself and his son into new scenarios of him and his daughter.

Or... She paused mid-inflation of the balloon stent. Possibly...was he hurting?

She thought back to the childhood he'd had, with one parent walking out and the other keep-ing him at arm's length emotionally. There were studies proving that children raised without touch or affection could very easily veer to-wards sociopathic tendencies. Maybe that was why Leon was such a good surgeon. No actual feelings were running through him.

She remembered his caresses from the night before, his whispered terms of endearment, the sweet-as-honey kisses he'd given her before they'd left the flat that morning.

Nah.

She gave the balloon a microscopic inflation, then paused again.

'Everything okay?' Autumn asked.

'Just ensuring the left heart ventricle isn't increased at too rapid a rate of knots,' she lied, trying to figure out something—anything—that would explain why Leon had responded so poorly to the news that he was having a daughter.

Maybe he was experiencing hormones by proxy.

To be honest, if she loved him—if she really loved him as she thought she did—she'd have to learn to shake this kind of thing off. They were going to spend a lifetime together. Everybody needed alone-time, right? Everyone had occasional 'moments'. Especially when their life was going to change for ever in about four and a half months.

Then again…

'It isn't like he doesn't have options,' Lizzy said, with a frustrated harrumph.

'Sorry?' Autumn looked at her, confused.

'Leon!'

'Do you mean about Grace's heart? Were you planning on isolating the shared aortic valve during surgery?'

Lizzy stared at her for a minute, then withdrew her instruments from the model.

'I don't think I can do this.'

'What? Of course you can.'

The two of them stared at the model of the babies for a moment, and then Lizzy burst out laughing. 'No—sorry. I can do the surgery. I just don't think I can do it with, you know…' she pointed at her belly '…things up in the air the way they are.'

Autumn threw a look over her shoulder, as if hoping an escape route would present itself. The look said one of the two of them was acting a little bit irrationally, and it wasn't Autumn.

'I mean, why won't he just make up his mind?' Lizzy threw up her hands. 'One minute he's all "marry me" and the next he's all "I've got surgery…can't talk." What sort of father-to-be does that?'

Autumn, who obviously had absolutely no idea what Lizzy was talking about, said, 'Most of the fathers-to-be that I deal with are worse than the mums.'

Lizzy sat with that nugget for a minute. 'Yeah. I suppose you're right. Women have a much more present reality to cope with.' She pointed again at her swelling belly.

Autumn nodded. 'They're powerless, aren't they? The men? And men like to fix things. This is one thing they have absolutely no control over and it makes some of them a bit bonkers.'

'Especially surgeon men,' Lizzy said, with a *know what I mean* look.

Autumn gave an *oh, yes, I do* nod, shared a complicit smile and asked, 'Want to talk about it?' in a way that said she'd be a sounding board, but wouldn't be interfering.

'No!' Lizzy huffed. 'Yes…' She gave herself a little shake. 'Actually, it'd be nice to have a woman to talk to. But not just yet. I need to let all this maddening Italian man business marinate for a bit.' Her eyes shot to the door as a group of doctors raced past. 'Erm… Mind if we keep this little incident to ourselves?'

'What goes on in the lab, stays in the lab.' Autumn locked her lips with an invisible key and threw it away.

Lizzy gave her a grateful smile. She liked this woman. She hoped whoever she was avoiding wasn't half as frustrating as Leon.

A tiny exchange from that morning's briefing flared in her mind. One between Giovanni and Autumn. They'd been comparing notes and had begun speaking over one another, and then, just as quickly, deferring to each other to go first. It had ended in a weirdly awkward stalemate during which neither had spoken but they'd kept looking into one another's eyes.

Hmm… Lizzy's mind began to whirr. It wasn't often she was so caught up in her own personal dramas that she failed to notice a burgeoning romance. 'Coffee date some time?' she asked.

'Will there be cake?' Autumn laughed, then put on a nonchalant expression. 'Seeing as we're in Rome, and all.'

Lizzy's smile widened. 'Absolutely. Until then…enjoy the lab!'

'I consider it my new home away from home,' Autumn said, already settling in front of a fresh model of the twins.

Right, Lizzy vowed as she set off to find Leon. If they were going to give this relationship a big dose of reality, maybe it was time they had their first proper fight.

* * *

Leon slid his key into the lock, hoping the occasional squeak his front door emitted wouldn't make a noise. It was late, and if Lizzy was asleep he didn't want to wake her.

'Hello, there.'

He knew in an instant that she'd caught his instinctive reaction—dismay—and also that he was in the doghouse.

'Don't worry. I'm making arrangements to stay at the hotel from tomorrow. Or,' she said, before he could protest, 'I can always go tonight. Don't worry about me.'

'I do worry about you, Lizzy. *Mea culpa*. I had surgeries.'

'Oh, I know. I'm not cross about that.'

He didn't have to ask her what she was actually cross about. It was written all over her face.

He'd shut her out.

It wouldn't have taken more than ten seconds to send a text saying he was held up. Telling himself it wasn't necessary, that she'd figure it out, was exactly the type of thing his mother would have done if she'd been out of sorts.

'*Scusi*, Lizzy. *Per favore.*'

He pressed his hands to his heart, on the brink of blaming it all on the day's surgical schedule getting away with him when he realised he owed her more than that. He owed her the truth.

'Don't move to the hotel. Stay. I had—how do you say it?—I had a blip.'

Lizzy screwed up her face, confusion taking over where there had previously been anger. 'What do you mean "a blip"?'

He sat down on the sofa beside her and took her hand in his. 'Seeing our daughter…knowing she was a she and not an it… I don't know… You think I'd be used to it. But because she's real…because she's *ours*… I suddenly felt inadequate.'

'What? What on earth would make you think that you, of all people, wouldn't be a great father?'

He shrugged. 'Conditioning, I guess.'

'You know your mother was wrong, right? She gave you bad advice about pretty much everything. No offence,' she hastily tacked on.

'Was she, though…?'

Leon wasn't defending her; he was genuinely trying to picture himself as a father. It was virtually impossible for him to picture it.

'You said so yourself, Lizzy.' He fanned his hand out across the immaculate flat. 'This place wasn't put together by someone who wanted a family.'

Lizzy gave him a hard stare, and after a moment said, 'I'm not going to try and talk you into having a baby you don't want, Leon. I told you that from the start. If you don't want me—'

He cut her off. 'That's not it at all. I do want you. Very, very much. And although I'm making a proper mess of it, I want our child, too, I just thought—'

'Oh, God.' Lizzy gave an exasperated sigh. 'You're not going to give me the "bad timing" talk, are you? Or—wait—is it the "it's not you it's me" talk?'

He gave her a sheepish smile. She was right on both counts.

Lizzy took her hand out of his and rearranged herself so she sat cross-legged on the sofa. She took a deep, shaky breath, then said, 'Did you ever know my father was emotionally abusive to my mother?'

Leon felt his heart slam against his chest. As if this dark chapter of her past were a physical assault on the woman he loved and therefore, by extension, an assault on him. 'No.'

'She couldn't do anything right. Not in his eyes anyway. No matter what the situation, he always found a way to twist it so that she was to blame. But do you know the one thing she did do right, despite being totally screwed up and having no self-confidence and a huge closet full of unfulfilled dreams?'

Leon shook his head.

'She raised me to want something different. And up until I met you I thought I'd turned out mostly okay.'

Leon flinched. He knew he deserved that. 'Lizzy, you've turned out so much more than okay.'

She tipped her head back and forth, clearly unwilling to accept the compliment. Her eyes welled up as she continued. 'She loved me so fiercely. Protected me from whatever she could. Guided me as best she could. Did she do a perfect job? Probably not. I've got issues. I rarely speak to my father. I find it almost impossible to visit my mother's grave. I prefer to keep my past to myself—as evidenced by the fact that I'm only telling you this now. I fell in love with a man who finds it every bit as hard to fall in love as I do.' She threw up her hands, then unexpectedly smiled. 'I'm flawed. But who isn't? And do you know what else? Our child probably will be, too.'

'No. Lizzy. She's perfect.'

'*Now* she is,' Lizzy gently corrected him. 'But she's not lived yet. She's not had her pigtails pulled, or tripped on the street in front of laughing children, or been shouted at, or—'

Leon waved his hands for her to stop. He understood what she was saying. They needed to be this child's buffer against the world. And if he wasn't going to be there for Lizzy, there was no way he could be there for their daughter.

A hunger to prove to her that he was more than the sum of his past gripped him. He'd boxed himself into a world of work and recuperation that allowed for little else. Lizzy had been the one woman to let in all that amazing light the rest of the world had to offer. Their child would let in so much more. If he let her.

'Here.'

Lizzy sat up straighter, as if physically repositioning herself in order to dig deeper into the conversation than either of them would have done five years ago. And she was right to do it. They weren't singletons with nothing but their professions to worry about. They were going to be parents in a few months. He'd asked her to marry him, for heaven's sake. This was their future they were talking about.

'I'm going to give you a quiz,' Lizzy said brightly. Too brightly.

'What kind?' He shifted round on the sofa so that they were facing one another.

'A "How Prepared is Anyone for Parenthood?" Quiz.'

He laughed. Considering the hundreds of variations of parents he'd seen through the years this should be interesting...

She peppered him with questions about nappies and breast milk and E-numbers in baby food, and the sort of shoes he thought they should buy, and how important having a first birthday party was, considering the child wouldn't remember it. Then, abruptly, she shifted tack. 'How are clouds built? Out of marshmallows or cotton balls?'

'Neither,' Leon said, a bit surprised that she didn't know. 'Clouds are made up of water vapour—'

Lizzy cut him off with a buzzer sound. 'You're answering a three-year-old. At bedtime. A three-year-old who wants a story. Let's try again. "Papà?"' She put on a little girl's voice. '"How are clouds built?"'

Leon tapped his chin, then answered. 'They're

built out of dreams, *cara*. That's why they come with silver linings.'

Lizzy nodded approvingly. 'Better.'

Leon ran his fingers along Lizzy's shoulder, then put his hand on her belly. 'Aren't you scared?'

'Terrified,' she answered, with a directness that, rather than frightening him, made him feel closer to her than he ever had. 'But I'll be less scared if I know I don't have to do it alone.'

'Right, then,' he said. 'Looks like I'm going to have to train myself to text when I'm going to be kept late at the hospital.'

'Old dog, new tricks?' Lizzy quipped.

'Something like that.' He laughed, giving her a soft kiss. And then, hand in hand, they went to bed.

CHAPTER THIRTEEN

LIZZY AND LEON were mid-chorus in the scrub room when Giovanni Lombardi walked in.

He looked between the pair of them: Leon mid-dance move at the scrub sink, Lizzy playing a rather exuberant air guitar.

'You two are full of the joys of life today,' Giovanni said, with a look that suggested he wasn't quite sure he trusted it.

They had told him about their pregnancy situation a few days earlier as a professional courtesy, after he'd found Lizzy asleep in the practice lab. He had appeared unsurprised, obviously having seen that Lizzy's floaty clothes wardrobe had pretty much become a clingy clothes wardrobe.

She must do that shop!

Giovanni, ever the gentleman, hadn't asked for details, merely an assurance that she was physically up to doing today's surgery—which, of course, he'd received. So, all in all, it had been a big week. Their first fight. Their first adult conflict resolution. Their first after-fight make-up session—extra-sexy. And now life-altering surgery on a little girl who still had all this glorious falling in love yo-yo ride yet to come.

'It's a big day.' Lizzy gave Giovanni a grin, taking a surgical gown down from the supplies shelf and laying it out on the sterilised counter. She grabbed a packet of plastic gloves and dropped them onto the sterile gown without touching them. Protocol was everything on any day in the surgical ward, but today it felt even more important.

'Are you observing or scrubbing in?' Leon asked his boss, switching his scrub brush to his other hand.

'Observing,' Giovanni said. 'With Autumn.'

There had been, if Lizzy wasn't mistaken, the tiniest bit of weight added to Autumn's name when he'd said it. Hmm…perhaps she and Leon weren't the only ones holding a secret set of love cards close to their chests.

'Things are going well with her?' Leon asked, oblivious.

Giovanni made a noise that was hard to interpret, then muttered something about having to check on how Gabrielle was doing with the anaesthetist.

Lizzy joined Leon at the sink, opening the package that contained her sterile nail brush, scrub spine and nail pick, laying each one out on the back of the specialised sink while she worked a few drops of scrub solution into a thick lather.

'You look like you're preparing for a bubble bath,' Leon said.

'If that's a suggestion for a post-operation date, I'm all for it.' Lizzy gave him a light hip-bump.

She couldn't see his lovely mouth because, as protocol dictated, he was already wearing his mask, but she could tell he was smiling from the crinkles fanning out alongside those gorgeous eyes of his. She, too, put her mask on, then began the detailed process of scrubbing in.

This felt good. Really good. Standing next to her man. With surges of pre-surgical adrenaline adding an extra bounce to her step. She'd pretty much lived in the practice lab for the past few days and now she felt prepared for anything. Especially with things so good between her and Leon.

If she'd thought she loved him before their little contretemps last week, she loved him even more now they'd talked it out. Treated one another with respect. Given each other the room to be frightened and assured one another they were not in this alone.

She gave herself a smug little mental pat on the back. Theirs was shaping up to be an actual grown-up relationship. Something she'd never made room for in her life. She obviously hadn't been given a stunning example by her parents, so this was an incredibly steep learning curve, but, yes, they were happy. And about to make medical history.

All in all, a pretty good way to start a day. Especially when she factored in the pastries they'd bought on the way into the hospital. *Scrumptious.* She hadn't told Leon yet, but she was already actively considering staying here in Rome rather than asking Leon to move to Sydney...

She pushed away those thoughts. Logistics could come later. They still had months to figure those out.

'Here she comes.'

Leon tipped his head towards the operating theatre where Gabrielle and her ever-increasing tummy were being wheeled in. She was already anaesthetised via an epidural, and it was reassuring to see her features, increasingly tense these past couple of weeks, relaxed and at ease. She was awake, and would be throughout the procedure. A small grin appeared as she caught sight of Lizzy and Leon at the window. She lifted her hand, already fitted with a drip catheter, and wiggled her fingers.

Lizzy felt a gratifying squeeze in her heart. It was that expression that always gave her an extra fire to care for her patients and protect them from any harm that might come their way. They were so vulnerable. So trusting. And it wasn't just one life Gabrielle had entrusted them with today—it was three.

'Ready?' Lizzy stepped back from the sink, her arms crooking into the surgical gown the scrub nurse was holding for her.

'As I'll ever be,' Leon replied, his eyes flashing with that same flare of brilliance that had first drawn her to him during their very first surgery together all those years ago.

They entered the surgical theatre.

'How're you feeling?' Lizzy asked Gabrielle. 'I'd give your hand a squeeze, but—' She held up her gloved hands.

'No, you do exactly what you have to do for

my little Hope,' Gabrielle said. 'We believe in you. And Dr Cassanetti, of course.'

Lizzy's eyes flicked to Leon's. He was shaking his head.

'It's all about Dr Beckley today, Gabrielle. I'm here as back-up. You've got one of the world's best surgeons here to help you, so your job is to lie back and relax.'

Gabrielle laughed. 'Relax? I'll try my best. At least I know I won't be moving. I can't feel a thing!'

'Sounds about right,' Leon said warmly. 'We've got you.'

He looked across at Lizzy, who somehow felt the words were meant for her as well. He had her back. He was there to be her support system. And knowing that meant the world.

'We'll all be putting our very best feet forward today, I promise you,' Lizzy assured her, before thanking the team for being there. Then she asked one of the surgical nurses to start the clock they used to time surgeries, gave Leon a nod to say that it was time for them to take their positions and, without any fanfare, the procedure began.

Time took on another quality as the first crucial keyhole incision was made. Though the entire procedure would take less than an hour, Lizzy knew that by the time they had finished it would feel as if the world had rotated on its axis. But the countless hours she, Leon and the team had spent in the practice lab were paying dividends. The dream team she and Leon had once been was well and truly back in action.

'How're Grace's stats?'

'Holding steady.'

'Mum? How are you doing?'

One of the obstetrics team in charge of Gabrielle gave a thumbs-up and Gabrielle herself, hidden behind a surgical drape, said she couldn't believe how lucky they were to have found St Nicolino's, and Leon and Lizzy, and Giovanni and Autumn. Then she began listing all her favourite nurses, and the puddings she had eaten that week, before rhapsodising about some deep-fried courgette flowers laced with truffled honey that her husband had brought her the other day from a street vendor.

Did they know she loved her husband? she asked. She loved him more than anyone or anything else in the world. That might change when the babies were born, of course, but who else would go out scouting for things she could eat? She hadn't been able to eat before today's operation and she was starving. Did stomachs rumble when there was an epidural?

Lizzy grinned at Leon. This was good. Having a relaxed, happy patient, a bit punch-drunk on the anaesthetic all factored into the feel-good environment critical to the kind of surgery that could so easily end in tragedy.

It was a precarious balance. Sharing the central aortic valve meant that each of the babies relied on the other's blood flow, and as Hope's blood flow was compromised by the underdevelopment of the left side of her heart, the strain would be felt by both girls.

Lizzy glanced up at the monitor, where she could now see a perfect image of Hope's heart. On the screen, of course, it was large, and showed all the details required to make the surgery a success. In reality, Hope's heart was the size of a large grape. And Lizzy was going to have to pierce through the thick wall of that heart with exacting precision, then guide the catheter through the chambers of the heart cavity into the left atrium—which was, at this point, about the size of a pea. She'd inflate the tiny balloon at the tip of the catheter before withdrawing the needle, touching absolutely nothing along the way.

No pressure, then…

She felt a scrub nurse reach up and pat her brow.

Yup. Things were getting serious.

Lizzy glanced around the room at all the concentrating medical professionals. They had the best team in the country here. Foetal cardiologists, obstetricians, imaging experts, maternal and foetal anaesthetists… The amount of brain power in this room could run a nation—but today they were saving a child's life. Without this surgical intervention Hope's chances of survival were limited. And as a result, so were Grace's.

'Are you ready?'

Lizzy looked into Leon's eyes, seeking that extra shot of confidence she needed to start the core elements of the procedure. She blinked once and saw trust. She blinked again and saw confidence. The third time she saw love. A rush of strength filled her with a tightly coiled burst of exacting energy. Precisely what she needed in this moment.

Apart from her voice, talking the team through her every move, the operating room was filled with little noise beyond the muted sounds of the equipment. Drips were in place. Extra pairs of hands were standing by if needed. Surgical nurses had stepped into place to hold each of Gabrielle's hands.

Lizzy glanced up to the observation deck and saw Giovanni lean forward, elbows on knees, cupping his chin in his hands as she prepared to make her life-changing move. Autumn was there, biting her lower lip. This surgery was as important for them as it was for her.

Lizzy looked back at the monitor, took in a deep, steadying breath, then began to offer Hope a better chance of survival...

Everything in Leon stilled as he watched the high-tech ultrasound images appearing on the screen across the room from him. Though this surgery was precisely the reason he'd flown Lizzy halfway across the world, he watched in awe as she inserted the catheter with such unerring confidence it was as if she'd done it a thousand times.

She had done it once. On a single child. The risks with Hope and Grace were so much higher that he doubted more than a handful of surgeons in the world would have risked it. But if she didn't try—if they, as a team, didn't try—it would effectively be giving up on Hope and

Grace. And giving up wasn't something they liked to do here at St Nicolino's.

He kept an eye on Grace's heart as Lizzy carefully inflated the tiny balloon that would open the stenotic aortic valve. The intervention would allow the left ventricle to grow properly, ensuring normal blood flow in the heart.

Lizzy carefully pulled out the needle, having inflated the balloon just enough, and after a few more minutes of removing surgical tools, said, 'And... Hope's got herself a happier heart. How're you doing, Mum?'

Gabrielle choked back a sob of relief. 'Is it done? Really?'

'All done.' Lizzy walked around the surgical drape so she could look at Gabrielle, whose eyes were brimming with tears. 'We just need to close up the small incision and you can go back to your room to be with Matteo.'

The closing team stepped into place and began the small but essential procedure. Out of the corner of her eye Lizzy could see everyone in the gallery clapping, giving one another high-fives and fist-bumps.

'He won't believe this,' Gabrielle said, now openly crying. 'He simply won't believe it. Our little girls... They have a fighting chance now.

Thank you. No other hospital would do this. We will owe you for ever.'

'No.' Lizzy shook her head. 'You owe your thanks to Dr Cassanetti. He's the one who rang me, so he's the one you should be thanking.'

Leon raised his hand in acknowledgement. Generous to a fault, Lizzy was. Talented, generous, fearless… They were all things he'd seen before in Lizzy, but never with the understanding that she had come from a home filled with fear. A home that had lacked paternal love and support—just as his had.

Medicine. An impassioned drive to help innocents have a better start in life. A fiercely guarded heart. Were those just a few of the invisible strings that had drawn them together?

Very likely. And doubtless there would be more.

They would also find things they completely disagreed on. Moral stances on world issues. Ethical decisions when it came to deciding which surgeries were and were not risks worth taking. Whether or not toast was actually edible if it was burnt.

But they'd stick by one another *because* of their differences, not despite them. And for the first time in his life the prospect of a complicated, messy life excited him.

'Catch up in twenty minutes?' Lizzy asked as she passed Leon on the way out of the theatre, while the team prepared to take Gabrielle to her room.

'Sure. But...' He furrowed his brow, trying to figure out what she was doing.

'I'm just going to nip out and get some air before we talk the Bianchis through the next steps.'

When she didn't reappear as promised, instinct guided him to her.

He pushed open the door to the hospital's south wing rooftop terrace and looked across the broad expanse of the healing garden Giovanni had commissioned a few years back. It had a pair of shaded loggias, and trees heavy with blossom. There were water features and private little nooks where patients or anxious family members could sit and read, have their lunch—or, in Lizzy's case, have a quiet little weep.

Her back was to him, but he could see the tell-tale shake he'd become familiar with in his years as a surgeon. The shoulders of someone desperately trying to keep deep emotion at bay, but ultimately failing.

He walked through a waft of orange blossom scent as he made his way towards her. Above them, on the higher west wing roof, a helicopter came in. He heard the calls of the emergency staff, barely audible above the whirr of the helicopter blades. It was an acute reminder of the fragility of life. Two lives had been saved today. Others, most likely, would be lost.

He sat down beside her, not saying anything. She gave his knee an acknowledging pat. He handed her a clean handkerchief. He hoped they were tears of relief, not sorrow. A release after weeks of pent-up will I/won't I fears.

After her breathing had steadied, he said, 'You were brilliant today.'

She pursed her lips.

'Take the compliment, *cara*,' he urged gently. 'I don't hand them out that often.'

She parted her lips to protest, then stopped herself, a look of surprise taking over from where the disbelief had just been. 'You don't, do you?'

He shook his head. 'Not a big fan.'

She screwed up her face. 'Of compliments? Who doesn't like compliments?'

He hitched up a shoulder in response. Him. He didn't. Words never stood as proof to him that people felt a certain way. Actions did. And today Lizzy had made good on her promise to deliver a faultless surgery.

'You're just like my father.'

'What?' He shook his head. 'Sorry. I don't see the link.'

She lifted her phone from the bench. The face of it was freshly cracked, as if it had been hurled in anger.

'You rang your father?'

'Yup,' she said tightly.

'Why?'

She scrubbed her fingers through her hair, tugged out her ponytail and then did it up again, so tightly it looked almost painful. 'It was stupid. I rarely ring him—I mean, apart from birthdays and stuff—but I thought...' Her voice caught in her throat. She waited until the wave of emotion had passed before she spoke again. 'You know he's a cardiologist, right?'

Leon nodded. 'A well-respected cardiologist.'

Lizzy scrubbed her hands over her face, then through her fingers admitted, 'I thought what I did today—what *we* did today—might make him proud.'

Leon pulled her hands down, giving her knuckles a kiss. 'It should have. Any parent would be bursting at the seams to know their child had just changed another child's chances of survival.'

She put on a deep voice and a disdainful expression. '"What a waste of time and money. The child will most likely die anyway. The pair of them, probably. You think you've done something worthy today? Think again, Elizabeth. Think again."' She looked across at Leon, tears pouring down her face. 'I should have known this was what would happen. It's what always happens when I call home to brag.'

'It's not bragging, Lizzy—'

She shook her head. 'In my father's eyes, it is. There doesn't seem to be a single thing I can do to win his respect!' She wheeled on Leon with a ferocity he'd never seen from her. 'Did you know the only reason I accepted the job back in Sydney was for him? To prove to him—up close and personal—that I was worth loving?'

He wanted to cut in. To tell her that she had always been worth loving, and that if she'd let him he'd prove it. But she wasn't receiving information right now, and he had long ago sworn he wouldn't make promises he couldn't keep.

She carried on detailing her father's cruel tirade, and as she did so Leon felt as if she were plunging a knife deeper and deeper into his gut. So, this was how she'd been raised. With scorn. Contempt. No matter what Lizzy had done, her father had done something better. The actions of an insecure man taking out his un-happiness with the world on the only two peo-ple who had ever shown him true loyalty: Lizzy and her mother.

Lizzy's tears, he realised, as he felt his heart shredded into strips, weren't of relief. They were of sorrow. Bone-deep sorrow because no matter what she did it might never be enough to win her father's pure, uncomplicated love. It was something he didn't seem capable of.

And in that instant Leon knew that he couldn't ever, *ever* subject his child to the sort of behav-iour ingrained in Lizzy as normal.

Lizzy gave an angry *'Grr...'* Then, 'I just want to fly home and have it out with him, you know? March him through Sydney, past every child who's now in kindergarten, or grade school, or learning to ski, or doing their first somersault, and say, *See that child? That child would be dead if it weren't for me!'*

There was rage in her voice. But more than that there was anguish. And hopelessness. He got it. He'd tried to please a man who had walked out on him through no fault of his. A man he'd made himself intentionally lose track of so that he'd never have to go through what Lizzy was going through now.

The only difference between him and Lizzy, he supposed, was that Lizzy still actually spoke to her father. But the truth was, no matter how far away his own father was, how distant they were, he knew his father lived in his heart. Snagging and cutting and reopening those childhood wounds at unexpected moments like these, when he had to fight like hell not to cut and run. These were the moments his father hadn't wanted any part of. Moments his mother would have used as proof that she was right to keep her emotions closed.

'What do you want me to do?' he asked.

'Nothing!' she snapped. 'You can't do anything to help, so just back off—all right? It's what you're best at, isn't it? Walking away when things are good? Well, let this stand as proof that you should've handed me my walking papers after the surgery.'

Leon bridled, but didn't say anything. She was hurting and lashing out. Hitting him where she knew it would hurt.

He sat with her a moment longer, then pressed

himself up to stand. 'How about I let the Bian-chis know you'll be down in a bit?'

She held up a hand, but didn't look at him. 'No. I'll speak with them. Give me five minutes and I'll be down.'

Leon didn't like walking away—not like this—but he knew she was right. In this in-stance there wasn't anything he could do.

A few splashes of cold water and a bit of freshly applied make-up later, Lizzy felt as though she'd reined in her feelings enough to face the Bian-chis.

When she got to their room she discovered that Leon hadn't, as per her request, waited for her to speak to the couple. The three of them were laughing about something, and when they all looked across at her as one, instead of re-laxing her, their camaraderie made her feel painfully isolated. Not so much Gabrielle and Matteo. They were innocents in this. It was Leon who was making her cross.

She'd asked him to wait.

Why was it that the men in her life steamroll-ered along without a care in the world about the feelings of the people who loved them? It wasn't as if she hadn't taken his feelings into consideration when she'd found out she was pregnant. She'd flown halfway around the world to tell Leon face to face that he was having a child. Sure, she hadn't done it with any particular grace or class, but she'd done it. She'd done what an honourable, decent person would do, regardless of the countless hoops she'd had to jump through.

She'd had to get a replacement—three, actually—to cover her long absence from the hospital. And that would have to be taken into account again, in a few months' time, when she actually had the baby. Not to mention that it was Leon's malfunctioning condom that had got them into this mess in the first place! Sure, she might've instigated things by looking completely and totally sizzling hot at the conference supper—even if she did say so herself. And she'd had just-in-case condoms, too. Reliable ones. But, no! They'd had to use Leon's.

And now she was carrying the baby of the one man in the world she'd ever loved. But today… Today she didn't like him very much. Especially right now.

'Dr Beckley.' Leon's smile was tentative as his eyes connected with hers. 'Good to see you. I was just telling the Bianchis we have some recordings of the sonograms if they want to send the audio and a few stills of their children's heartbeats to family back home. Apparently, their phones haven't stopped ringing.'

Oh, terrific, she thought sourly, with a barely contained eye-roll. Lucky Bianchis. *They* had families who *cared.* Families who celebrated when it was appropriate. Families who celebrated when—

She stopped herself. She was being horrid. This wasn't her. This wasn't the woman she wanted to be or the doctor she had trained herself to become. More to the point, this type of reactive behaviour and self-sabotage wasn't anywhere near the woman she wanted to be when she became a mother.

It wasn't anyone's fault—not even her own—that her father was a jackass. But it could still make her mad.

She tried to shoot Leon a not entirely apologetic look for being so awful to him up on the roof, but he wasn't looking at her. He was doing what any good doctor offering antenatal care to a woman who had just gone through exceedingly rare in utero surgery should. Focussing on his patients.

Forcing herself to regroup, she managed to

tag on to the end of Matteo asking Leon what happened next.

She jumped in. 'The babies are in the best possible place right now. Gabrielle's beautiful natural incubator. There is a chance, of course, that Hope will need surgery shortly after she's born, depending on how long we can keep the babies where they are. She could outgrow the stent we put in today—which, big picture, is a good thing, because it would mean a longer gestational period, but as you know the risks are high.'

She rattled off a few things they'd been through before, including gestational diabetes and pre-eclampsia, then realised she had gone on for far too long and wrapped up quickly. 'But ultimately we're hoping it all goes like clockwork.'

She faltered as she saw their expressions shift from slightly confused to very confused, and then, more horrifyingly, to worried.

'Ah, *scusi*, Dr Beckley...?'

Leon was speaking in his 'polite' voice. The one that carried one very clear emotion—disappointment.

'We were talking about how to fry courgette flowers with ricotta.'

Lizzy gulped. 'You were...?'

'*Si.* Matteo's family are big foodies, and after these two enjoyed the *zucchini fritti* from Mercato Testaccio, they wanted to know if they were easy to make.'

'And are they?' she asked, at a complete loss as to how she'd got so caught up in her own problems she'd forgotten to focus on the people today was really about.

'Very. If you take your time and pay attention,' he added pointedly.

Even though his words hadn't entered her gut with the same cruel twist her father's words always did, Lizzy felt they were laced with the same disapproving venom. Her insecurities, having been contained as best she could these past few months, threatened to take over.

Leon thought she was careless. He thought she'd behaved poorly. He thought she wasn't worthy of the responsibilities he had given her. And, more devastatingly, he couldn't bear the idea that she was the woman who was going to be the mother of his child.

Completely flustered, she began explaining to the Bianchis about her brain being still caught up in the surgery, which she was so pleased about she'd not really been able to take anything else in. But she could feel an uncomfortable heat in Leon's gaze, and as quickly as she could she excused herself, assuring the Bianchis that she'd be back later in the afternoon to do another sonogram on the babies, so that they would have all sorts of recordings to send to family and friends.

'To anyone at all!'

She hot-rodded it to the changing rooms, almost knocking Autumn over in the process.

'Everything okay?' Autumn asked, her Scottish burr making the words sound utterly musical.

It was soothing. A foolish idea popped into her head. Wouldn't it be lovely to hear Autumn tell her a story? A fairy tale in which everything ended perfectly. Where the hero and heroine held one another close and promised each another a lifetime of joy, and the baddies melted away into little puddles of insignificance.

It would, of course, be completely ridiculous to ask. Even so, it would be so lovely to have someone outside her bubble of hysteria to speak with. Someone who had some perspective. Maybe she should ask her advice on what she thought a single, pregnant woman who had just snapped the head off her baby daddy and didn't really know if she was coming or going should do.

'Have you ever acted like a complete idiot in front of a patient?' she asked instead.

'Absolutely,' Autumn replied without a moment's hesitation. 'It's inevitable, given what we do.'

'What did you do about it after?'

The tiniest, most cowardly part of her was hoping that Autumn would say that she'd pretended it had never happened and life went on to be perfectly perfect.

'I marched right back in there, apologised, and set things straight.' Autumn pushed her hands into her scrubs pockets. 'If you deal with it straight away I find most patients are pretty forgiving. They want to believe we're extraordinary, but there's a part of them that takes comfort from the fact that we, too, are mortal. In other words you can make mistakes in your bedside manner, but you can't in Theatre.'

Lizzy hung her head. Yeah… That sounded about right. She looked back up at Autumn, whose green eyes were warm with compassion.

'Our patients come to us when they're vulnerable, scared, and have absolutely no control over what is happening in their own bodies.

Being entrusted with their hope is an equally scary thing, but I'd rather be in my shoes than theirs. Wouldn't you?'

Lizzy nodded, grateful that Autumn's question was rhetorical and, mercifully, had been delivered without judgement.

They made another vague plan to 'do coffee' before Lizzy did an about-face and headed back to the Bianchis' room, where—thankfully— there was no sign of Leon. She apologised from the bottom of her heart. Even squeezed a few laughs out of them by re-enacting the time she'd dressed up as a unicorn one Halloween, only to get her horn stuck when the lift doors were closing, so the fire brigade had to free her.

Now for the harder part, she thought, as she forced herself to head to Leon's office. She owed him an apology for lashing out at him. For taking his appearance in the Bianchis' room personally. He was a doctor above anything— especially here at the hospital—and of course that meant his patients came first.

She heard him before she saw him. It sounded like a one-way conversation, so most likely he was on the phone. It couldn't be that private, because the door was open, so she hovered beside it, waiting for the call to end.

Thirty seconds later she wished she'd asked Autumn for that story instead.

'…and if my daughter's born here in Italy, her citizenship will be Italian, not Australian, right?' Leon was asking. He murmured a few 'I sees' and a couple of 'Interestings'.

Lizzy tried to tell herself the question was a perfectly natural one for him to ask. Even so… prickles of fear ran along her skin.

'So, no one can take her away, then?'

Lizzy's hands flew to her throat, where her heart had lodging too tightly for her to breathe. What was he doing? Was he trying to keep their little girl here? Trying to gain custody before she was even born?

Leon's voice had turned very serious now. 'And how quickly can I apply for parental responsibility? *Si?* Straight away. And the mother's parental responsibility is automatic? I see. *Va bene.*'

Blood was roaring so loudly in Lizzy's brain that she couldn't hear any more.

Leon was trying to take control of their child before she'd even given birth to her. It was precisely the sort of thing her father would have done. Precisely the kind of future she'd vowed her daughter would never, ever have.

So, she did the only thing she could think of. She ran.

CHAPTER FOURTEEN

LEON WAS BESIDE HIMSELF. He couldn't find Lizzy anywhere. She wasn't answering his calls or his texts. She wasn't on the roof garden or in the flat. He'd careered around Rome on his scooter, revisiting the places they'd been together in the vain hope that he would find her. He'd even rung the airlines who had flights to Sydney that evening, only to be informed there was no chance he could get access to any flight manifest.

When he got back to the hospital he ran straight to the Bianchis' room, only to be told he had just missed her.

'Literally,' Gabrielle said, clearly clocking the frustration he didn't have the energy to disguise. 'Maybe five minutes ago?' She looked at her husband who nodded. It had been about that.

Leon's instinct was to page her on the hospital's PA system. Call Security and have them stop her. Or do more of what he'd been doing and run around with his eyes peeled for a glimpse of that singular swathe of straw-blonde hair. Surely he could catch up with a pregnant woman?

He turned to go but the Bianchis were feeling chatty. Wreathed in smiles, the couple told him how Lizzy had been so kind. She'd made both audio and video recordings from the surgery, and done a fresh sonogram just twenty minutes earlier, so that they had plenty of updates to share with their families back home.

'And what happened then?'

'And then she left,' Matteo said, hoicking himself up onto his wife's bed and pulling her into a cuddle. 'Said she'd check in tomorrow.' He grinned at his wife, then dropped a kiss onto her forehead.

The gesture doubled Leon's need to find Lizzy. He wanted what they had. The automatic instinct to protect each other. To care. To be there even in this kind of unbelievably frightening time and still find a way to line it with hope. The kind of hope he should have invested in a future with Lizzy a long time ago.

He'd got it all wrong on the roof.

He should've held her. Supported her. Told her that her father had absolutely no idea what he was talking about and that she was one of the most talented, amazing women he'd ever met. But most of all, he should've just been there for her.

She didn't need the situation to be fixed. No one was ever going to be able to change her father. But he could change himself. He could admit that he loved her. Admit that it scared him because love was like that first surgical cut. You didn't always know what you were getting, but you did it anyway because you had to. And that was where he was. At the do I/don't I crossroads.

'Did she say where she was going?'

They both shook their heads in the negative.

'And how did she seem?' he asked, trying and failing to ratchet down the intensity of his request. 'You know…in herself?'

Gabrielle and Matteo shared a look. One that indicated they had definitely talked about Lizzy and, very possibly, about him.

He gave up on being polite.

'Per favore…' He put his hands in the prayer position. 'Did she give any indication as to where she was going? I must find her.'

Gabrielle squealed and grinned triumphantly at Matteo. 'I *knew* it! I told you, didn't I? The

baby may or may not be his, but he loves her!'
Her eyes widened and she clapped her hand over her mouth.

Matteo shot him an apologetic smile. '*Scusi, Dottore.* My wife—she has far too much time on her hands, so she makes up little stories about everyone.'

Leon felt more exposed than he ever had in front of a patient—but, in another first, he found he didn't really care. Role reversal at its finest.

'No,' he admitted, priming himself for what he needed to say to Lizzy. 'You're right. I love her.'

'And the baby?' Gabrielle held her breath.

'Mine,' he confirmed, with a swell of pride gripping his chest so fiercely he knew what he had to do.

He ran to the nurses' desk, took the phone they used for the public address system and dialled in a code.

Lizzy cocked her head to one side.

Had that been—?

Her heart skipped a beat.

It was Leon on the PA system. He was calling a Code Aquamarine.

The colour he used to describe her eyes.

She was transported back to one particularly perfect bubble bath they'd taken together in her tiny New York studio. It had been early days for their internships and their relationship. She frowned. If you could even have called it that. They'd just led their very first in utero surgery as a team. Twin-to-twin transfusion syndrome. It had been a resounding success and they had left the hospital feeling on top of the world.

They'd walked to her place, grabbing some pizza and some ice cream on the way. Once there, they'd filled her tub with citrus-scented bubbles and sloshed around kissing, relaxing and reliving the surgery, revelling in how well they'd worked together. The dream team.

He had kissed her bubble-coated fingertips and told her that if he was ever floundering, if he ever needed to feel as positive as he did in that moment, he would commandeer the hospital's PA and call a Code Aquamarine.

She'd locked that moment in its own compartment inside her heart. It was, she believed, the closest he'd ever come to telling her that he loved her. She'd almost blurted out that she loved him, but knowing somewhere deep inside her that their time in New York was exactly that, she'd stayed silent.

So, like any career girl intent on climbing the ladder rather than walking down the aisle, she'd laughed and pointed out the flaws in his plan. She might not be in that hospital, for one.

He'd snorted and said, 'As if!'

And, of course, he'd been right. Because here she was, seven years later, feeling more torn that she'd ever felt in her life. And where had she sought refuge? The waiting room of the emergency department.

It was the best place to put things into perspective. Parents were bringing their children in, often in tears, as they sought help for a broken arm, or a fever that wouldn't go away, or a cut on the forehead from a run-in with a countertop. She felt their pain by proxy, itching to take it away, and almost physically felt their relief as one of her colleagues took the child in their arms and said, yes, they would help. Of course they would help.

The ones that really got to her, of course, were those terror-stricken parents racing in with a child in their arms, limp or screaming, clearly in need of immediate assistance. Those were the ones who got her back on her feet, adding herself to the 'pit crew' in the ED, proactively taking away both the physical and emotional pain the family were enduring and with it her own pain...whatever it had been.

But this time nothing had moved her from her seat.

She sat, her hands on her stomach, concentrating all her energies on her child—a baby who was little more than the odd flutter of butterfly wings in her belly—and praying for some sort of sign that would tell her what to do. Stay? Go? Endure the pain of loving someone who didn't love her as perfectly as a Prince Charming, knowing that without the lows there couldn't be the highs of making love, swapping ice cream cones, or sharing a secret smile in the operating theatre. The moments that made her world feel perfect.

Or, in Leon-speak, aquamarine.

Until this very moment the code had completely slipped her mind.

Because, she snippily reminded herself, *he'd never needed her before*. And the only reason he wanted her now was to make sure she didn't leave the country before he could take their baby away from her.

Or... The tiniest ember of hope sprang to life in her chest. Or maybe he'd realised he didn't feel whole without her...

Unable to put herself through any more emotional turmoil—picturing herself being handed over to police custody until she gave birth had a way of tying a girl in knots—she pulled out her phone and texted him. As Autumn had more or less said, it was better to face one's mistakes head-on, deal with the consequences, then move on.

Relief flooded Leon's chest the moment he saw her, tucked away in a corner of the ED waiting room. Why on earth was she there?

'Amore mio.' He dropped to his knees and took her hands in his. 'You scared me.'

'Why?'

There was wariness in her voice. That same self-protectiveness she'd worn like a shield when she'd told him she was pregnant.

'I couldn't find you. I wanted to talk.'

She stiffened. 'What about?'

He looked round the waiting room. It was relatively quiet, but it wasn't where he wanted to have *this* talk with *this* woman.

He glanced at his watch. 'Let's go out.'

She looked at him as if he were mad. 'I'm not going *anywhere* until you tell me whether or not my rights as a mother are protected.'

What the hell…? 'Your rights are precisely what I've been trying to figure out.'

She shook her head, not understanding.

'I've been researching what our child's legal rights are if she's born here—'

Lizzy abruptly stood up, her eyes blazing. 'Don't you think for one second you're getting sole custody of our daughter.'

For a second time the oxygen left his lungs. 'Lizzy, what are you planning?'

'I don't know yet,' she said, her chin jutting out, eyes blazing with defiance.

He caught the tiniest shake in her hands as she protectively knitted them together over the curve of her belly.

'But I know what you're trying to do. Get sole custody. I heard you on the phone.'

Compassion replenished his energy stores. She'd got it so wrong. His instinct was to pull her in close, hold her tight, but she was radiating anger and cuddling was definitely not on the cards. Yet.

'What exactly did you hear?'

'You were talking on the phone to someone—a lawyer, I presume—about whether or not you could have custody of the baby.' Her hands shifted protectively over her stomach.

He knew he shouldn't laugh at the misunderstanding. That was never a good way to react to an angry woman—especially an angry woman carrying your child. But huge blasts of relief and joy and, yes, love, were obliterating all the core-deep fear that had, mercifully, led him to her, each step opening his heart wide to their relationship and all its inevitable ups and downs.

He wanted it all. The laughter, the joy, the pain, the trust. But most of all he wanted the love he knew would only grow stronger. So, instead of laughing at her mistake, he crowded his myriad emotions into a soft smile and was met, unsurprisingly, with a defensive glare. She looked proud, brave, fiercely protective— everything he'd imagined she would be when their child was finally born. Everything he hoped she'd embody as a mother.

'Lizzy, I didn't want to do this here, but… I was talking to an immigration lawyer about you.'

He could almost see the flames stoking her fury.

'Why would you need to do that?'

'Because I don't want you to leave.'

Again, that defiant tilt to her chin presented itself. 'You don't get to tell me what to do.'

'I know. Which is why I am asking, right here, right now, in the centre of the emergency department, if you would do me the honour of being my wife.'

'You've got to stop asking me that when you don't mean it!' she said automatically, and then she looked at him—really looked at him.

He watched her as what she saw caused her breath to hitch. He knew his eyes were alight with something she hadn't seen before. Commitment. Pure, unswayable, solid-as-a-rock commitment. He'd felt the transition happen somewhere between the roof, the Bianchis' room and the moment when her text had come through. The one that had said, I'm here.

He loved Lizzy. With every fibre of his being. He wanted her. He wanted to be a father to the baby girl she was carrying and, if they were blessed, all the other babies yet to come.

'I want you to stay. Here. As my wife. If you'd like that, too. That's why I was speaking to the lawyer. To see what we needed to do for you to stay here. Legally. Beyond the Bianchis' surgery. It's up to you, obviously, but if you don't want to go back to Sydney, it's possible. I've spoken with Giovanni. He's happy to offer you a job here. You can live with me. We can move

flats, if you like. Move cities. Countries. Whatever it takes, Lizzy. I want to do whatever it
takes to give you and our child a happy, loving life.'

She shook her head, clearly trying and failing
to match up what she'd heard him say on the
phone with what he was asking now. 'No. You
were talking about the baby. How you wanted
to keep her here.'

'*And* you!'

She shifted her feet, the tension in her shoulders giving a little. 'Really?' Her eyes narrowed,
and her shoulders inched back up to her ears.
'Not just until the baby's born?'

Leon gave in to the urge to laugh. He clearly
wasn't going to get an answer to his proposal
just yet. Not without a long talk.

'I wanted to find out how to get you an Italian passport.'

'Why would I need one of those?'

'It might be handy for when you travel with
our daughter. It would also help if you want to
work here. But if you'd rather be in Sydney,
there are ways to make that happen, too.'

She frowned. 'So...you weren't finding out
ways to keep me here against my will?'

Now he really did have to laugh. 'Lizzy, I love

you. I want to do everything in my power to make you happy. To write our own history. One where you don't need your father's approval. Or mine, for that matter. One where you realise how amazing you are. How strong. How resilient. And how very much I love you.'

Her features softened enough to reveal the anxiety hidden in the creases of anger she'd been holding tight. 'And would that make you happy? Is that why you called the code?'

'Lizzy, you are the key to my happiness. You make my world a richer, better, much more interesting place to be. More than it could ever have been if I'd kept myself closed off the way I was taught.'

She put her hands to her belly and frowned. 'I'm hungry. I can't think until I've had something to eat.'

'Then let's go.' He held out a hand and pointed towards the exit.

She gave him a wary look. 'The canteen's just upstairs.'

'*Per favore,* Lizzy. My gorgeous, infuriating, deeply talented *pompelmo*… You're safe with me. We can leave a message at the nurses' desk, if you like. But let's go somewhere we can talk. Properly.'

She dithered, shifted her feet, looked any-where but at him, until finally she looked him straight in the eye. 'Okay, fine. But let's go to the flat via the deli. And that pastry shop—the one with the pistachio thingies. If I'm going to be subject to all these...' she scrubbed at the air over her swelling belly '..."emotions"... I'd rather do it away from the public eye.'

'As you wish, *amore*.'

He offered her his hand. She stared at it and then, to his surprise, took it.

'Shall we take the scenic route?' she surprised herself by asking.

Leon gave her a courtly half-bow. 'By all means.'

She realised as they walked that she wanted to look at Rome from a different angle. Not through a tourist's eyes, but from the perspective of someone who lived here.

Could she picture herself pushing a baby carriage through the higgledy-piggledy streets?

Yes.

Could she imagine Leon popping their little girl on his shoulders when her pudgy toddler legs were tired?

She threw him a secret sidelong glance, taking in his solid shoulders, his strong arms, and the way he walked so that none of the countless tourists bumped into her as they wove their way through the busy streets.

Yes. She could, actually.

She looked down at his left hand. Bare. Occasionally brushing hers. Making trills of response run through her body whether she wanted them or not.

Yes, she realised with a jolt. Finally, at long last, she could picture a wedding ring on his hand.

Which, of course, set off a ream of entirely different questions.

Should she keep her house?

Would it be lonely here?

She'd miss her housemate and her colleagues, of course, but her life pretty much revolved around her patients and that would be no different here. And Byron had his pilot, so...

Leon stopped at a street stall and bought two *arancini*. After they'd eaten, they continued to walk in a new but comfortable silence as they gathered their thoughts. She felt as if she needed to reach a decision before they got to his flat, because whatever it was she decided would be final.

The choice, she realised, was a simple one.

Did she want to risk giving her heart to Leon, knowing the baby that linked them for ever could grow up in the kind of happy family she'd never had? Or did she want to raise their child the way Leon's mother had? Alone. Too protective. So frightened of being hurt that her world would close in around her and, more to the point, around her daughter, excluding any possibility of love.

The answer was glaringly obvious.

Just then they turned a corner, and there was the Trevi Fountain, crowded as ever with families and couples throwing in coins, making wish after wish.

Leon gave her hand a squeeze and asked, 'Did you know it's still fed by aqueduct? For almost two thousand years Romans have gathered water from here.'

Lizzy shook her head in disbelief.

'Astonishing, isn't it?' Leon continued. 'To think something so beautiful—a frivolity at first glance—has endured as much history as it has. You know…' He held her away from him for a moment and looked at the fountain and then at her. 'I think the water's the same colour as your eyes.'

Lizzy shot him a look. Was he talking in metaphors? Saying *she* was a frivolity?

'War, famine, droughts, revolution—' Leon's list was long. 'It had to be shut down recently to be restored. It felt—' He laughed to himself. 'I know it sounds ridiculous, because it's so touristy, but it felt like the city wasn't completely alive without it. You know…?'

She nodded, still not entirely sure she was meant to be taking all this at face value. She pulled the analogy back to herself. The two years she'd spent with Leon had been the most vital, thrilling, dynamic years of her life. Since they'd been apart she'd never really ever felt the same. Like Rome with its fountain, she had felt as if something was missing. And that something was Leon.

Her heart doubled its cadence. This was her chance. An open door. A step away from her dark, unhappy past to make a fresh start.

Leon was studying the fountain with such intensity she was pretty sure he was mulling over the same questions. Hoping against hope that he was making the right call by asking her to share his life with him.

'Do you know the secret to the coins?' Leon

asked, digging in his pocket and showing her a few.

Again, she shook her head.

'You can throw in one, two or three.'

'And that has different meanings?'

He nodded. 'One coin means you wish to return to Rome.'

'And two?'

His eyes flickered with heat. 'Two coins means you wish to fall in love with an attractive Italian.'

'And I suppose that means you?'

He gave one of those careless shrugs of his, but now she saw all the things she hadn't before. Things she'd been too busy protecting her own heart to notice. She saw his vulnerability. His strength of character. His moral compass. And, most of all, she saw that he truly did love her. That he wanted this to work. For them to be a family.

'Are there any more options?' she asked, her voice barely audible above the noise of tourists laughing, telling one another their wishes and leaving it up to the fountain to decide whether or not they came true.

'Yes.' He took a step closer to her and held up a third coin. 'Three coins means you're wishing to come to Rome, find love and marry a handsome Italian.'

The space between them diminished. Lizzy's heart pounded against her ribcage. 'And are there statistics on any of these wishes being granted?'

He shook his head. 'Only for the lucky ones.'

'Do you think we're lucky?' she asked, her heart brimming with a level of hope she had never once let herself feel.

'Si, amore,' he said, ducking his head to hers, his lips brushing against her lips as he said, 'I think we're very lucky.'

And with that they turned their backs to the fountain, as tradition dictated, and she plucked three coins from his hand and threw them into the fountain.

CHAPTER FIFTEEN

'You look beautiful.'

Lizzy beamed at her reflection in the mirror, then back at Byron, who had 'hitched a ride' on his boyfriend's plane. 'D'you think?'

He rolled his eyes. 'Of course I think! You're going to have to trust your man of honour.'

'Trust you to what, exactly?' she giggled.

'Trust me to not let you loose on the streets of Rome looking like a ragamuffin!'

They laughed, and sighed, and caught one another's eyes in the full-length mirror Leon had bought expressly for this day. He had wanted her to have everything she wanted exactly where she wanted it, for this, their wedding day, and much to her surprise she had realised she wanted to get ready here, in the rooftop flat that had undergone quite a transformation over the past few weeks.

The waiting-room-style seats had been replaced by big sofas, good for a snooze or curling up and reading a book—also good for spills. The balcony had been baby-proofed. The second guest room had been turned into a nursery, its walls painted a soft natural green that made it feel as though you were walking into an enchanted sun-dappled woodland where the sole purpose was to protect and nurture the little girl growing inside her.

'I look fat!' She laughed.

'You look stunning,' Byron countered. 'You've got that pregnancy glow down pat.'

She gazed at herself. Her body was still vaguely unfamiliar to her, but she had to admit the lace and ultra-soft linen maxi-dress with a deep V cut down the back made her feel as beautiful as Leon did when he held her in his arms each night.

Her eyes dropped to her stomach, then to her engagement ring. The princess cut aquamarine jewel stood proud on the band of diamonds, looking as if it had been on her finger for ever. Today it would be united with a wedding band. A ring that would symbolise her lifelong commitment to Leon and their child.

Her hands swept over the taut, increasingly large ball that was their baby girl. Genevieve, they'd decided in the end. For her mother.

'I wish—' An unexpected rush of emotion balled in her chest as her heart lurched up into her throat.

'I know, honey,' Byron soothed. 'I wish your mum could see you, too.'

'Do you think I'm a bad person for not inviting my father?'

Byron shook his head. 'You said you and Leon had talked about it loads. Weddings are different things for different couples. Yours is about joy—not obligation. Yours is about choice.'

She nodded, blinking back tears, desperately trying not to mess up her carefully applied make-up. 'You're right. A real father doesn't do his utmost to make his child feel horrible about herself.' She drew in a shaky breath and managed to find a smile that made it all the way to her eyes. 'Today is about celebrating everything that's good about me and Leon and this little tyke.' She rubbed her hands on her belly, feeling the soft lace of her gown shift as she did. 'Oh! She just kicked.'

Byron's face lit up as she took his hand and pressed it to her stomach. 'Oh, wow. I'm definitely going to have to get to Rome more often. I don't want to miss this little one's life as she grows up.'

She gave him a grateful smile. 'Thanks for coming. And you know we'll come to Sydney every now and again?'

Byron laughed. 'I know you, missy. You'll come when there are some good surgeries on the board. And I'm guessing they're going to have to be pretty spectacular to get you away from that gorgeous fiancé of yours.'

Lizzy grinned. 'He is pretty cute, isn't he?'

'*Cute?*' Byron screeched. 'The man's a bloody catwalk model! And a world-class surgeon.' He gave her a hug. 'Well done, you. You deserve every gorgeous molecule of him.'

Lizzy's phone buzzed. 'Do you mind...?' she said.

Byron grabbed the phone from the bed and handed it to her. Lizzy frowned.

'Something wrong?' he asked.

'No, it's—it's the hospital number. I thought it might be Leon.'

'You said he was at the hospital, right?'

'Yes. He was going to pop in on the Bianchis before we went to the church.'

Five minutes later Lizzy was out of her dress and on the street, flagging down a taxi. '*Per favore*, St Nicolino's,' she said as Byron climbed in beside her. '*Pronto.*'

Byron elbowed her in the side. 'Check you out, Little Miss Italy.'

She grinned. 'That's Little Miss Almost *Mrs* Italy to you.' Her smile dropped from her face. 'Oh, gosh...'

'What?'

'This means I won't be getting married.'

'Seriously? You think it'll take that long?'

She gave him a solid stare and tried to shrug it off. 'Gabrielle has just had an eclampsic convulsion.'

Byron pulled a face. He knew what that meant. The involuntary contraction of muscles meant the babies needed to be delivered *now*.

'Gabrielle's health is on the line every bit as much as the health of the conjoined twins,' Lizzy said, even though she knew they both knew the score.

'Have they given her magnesium sulphate?'

Lizzy nodded, rerouting her mental energies into the operating theatre and away from the church.

Eclampsia was rare, but there was a small risk of permanent disability or brain damage from the convulsions and, if not treated immediately, it could mean both the mother's and the babies' lives were at severe risk.

'Can you ring the church, Byron? Let them know?'

'You've still got an hour. You might be able to make it.'

Lizzy gave him a look.

Byron promised to ring the church as soon as they got to the hospital.

In the end, they were both partly right.

The intensity of the scenario at the hospital demanded that Lizzy and Leon work in perfect synchronicity.

Gabrielle had had her seizure during Leon's morning visit. It happened sometimes, the total absence of signs that eclampsia was looming.

The babies were at thirty-one weeks. They'd been hoping for at least a couple more, but now Gabrielle's health was at risk as well there was no choice but to deliver the babies today.

Matteo was gowned up and holding his wife's hand as Leon prepared to make the first crucial incision, and he apologised once again for the timing. 'We are so sorry to have interrupted your wedding.'

Lizzy shook her head, gloved hands held up, ready for whatever she might be needed to do. 'Honestly, this is more important. Besides,' she added, trying to add a bit of brightness to the tense atmosphere, 'bringing your girls into the world today is like an early wedding present.'

Leon agreed. 'It's these two little girls who helped bring us back together again, so it makes sense that they should want to be part of our big day.'

Lizzy looked across the surgical table, her eyes cinching with her future husband's, and smiled. She hadn't thought of it that way. How huge a role Hope and Grace had played in their lives. Without them— She shook her head and any other thoughts away. Here and now was where she both wanted and needed to be.

Up in the gallery Byron gave her a thumbs-up. Down here on the surgical floor both Giovanni and Autumn were gowned up and standing ready to help if anything went wrong. But, because Leon was doing what he did best, the C-section went like clockwork, and before any of them could fully grasp what had happened Matteo was holding his little girls in his arms, then handing them to his wife. Both of them were disbelieving that these tiny, practically perfect babies that they had seen so many times on imaging screens were finally out here in the real world.

'Looks like you've got about four kilos of baby,' Leon said, once each of the parents had had a chance to kiss and hold their children.

As they'd been born prematurely, they still had a long road ahead—and, of course, there was the complicated separation surgery Giovanni and Autumn would helm once the little ones had developed more.

There wasn't any need to put in a new stent straight away, Lizzy was relieved to see, but the girls would need to be under close scrutiny in the NICU as their lungs developed, their bodies gained a bit more weight and they were better able to regulate their own temperatures.

Mercifully, Gabrielle seemed to be all right, but she, too, would be under Leon's close care. The list of post-operative problems after eclampsia wasn't pretty. But Gabrielle had a core of strength. One that would only grow stronger now that she'd kissed and held the babies she'd been carrying all these months.

'Will we be able to hold them again soon?' Gabrielle asked, her mother's instincts already at full throttle.

'Of course,' Leon assured her. 'You'll be able to be with them every day, but for now let us look after *you*.'

'Are you going to be with them too?' she asked.

Lizzy nodded, her smile deepening as she felt Leon's hand slip round her waist as he joined her by the bedside.

'And Drs Lombardi and Fraser. In fact, Autumn and Giovanni are getting the twins settled into their incubator now.'

'So they're not alone?' Matteo asked.

'Absolutely not. They'll never be alone,' said Leon. 'Right now, your job is to rest, Gabrielle. If you or the babies need us, we're only a phone call away.'

Lizzy shot him a look. 'Why? Where are we going?'

He gave her a cheeky grin. 'You'll see.'

The moment Lizzy entered the church, Leon knew he was in the right place, at the right time, doing exactly the right thing.

The flowers they'd organised had been left in place along with another wedding party's flowers, so now, a few hours later than planned, as Lizzy walked towards him, it was as if she were Eve, walking through a Roman Garden of Eden.

He knew it was ridiculous, but he felt like the very first man ever to have got married. To have loved this deeply. To have been filled to the brim with the knowledge that his life was going to be so much richer for having his wife in it.

Would it all be smooth sailing from here on out? Probably not. They each bore the bumps and nicks and scars of lives that could have been kinder to them, but they'd both come out stronger in the end. Stronger and more resilient, now they knew they had someone they could turn to.

When she reached the altar in front of their friends, a smattering of hospital staff and, of course, Lizzy's best friend from home, Byron, who was at her side, Leon took her hands in his. They stood there beaming at one another as the celebrant said whatever it was he said— they weren't really paying attention, just staring into one another's eyes, seeing nothing but possibility, nothing but light, nothing but joy.

They both had to be prompted to repeat their vows, and when, at long last, they were given licence to mark the beginning of their married life with a kiss, they did so with relish.

'I love you, Dottore Signora Cassanetti,' said Leon, and nuzzled into her neck, dropping a kiss in that perfect nook between her chin and her ear.

'I love you too,' she said, happily walking back down the aisle to the applause of their colleagues and friends.

'Fancy a honeymoon in Rome?' Leon asked with a cheeky grin.

'I fancy a lifelong honeymoon in Rome,' Lizzy answered, then grinned and gave his hand a tug. 'But first…do you want to go to the NICU?'

Leon nodded. He had married the perfect woman for him. And today had been the very best day to begin their lives together as husband and wife. He couldn't wait for the rest of their marriage to reveal itself, tantalising morsel by morsel. Just like the perfect Italian meal…

* * * * *

LET'S TALK
Romance

For exclusive extracts, competitions
and special offers, find us online:

- ◼️ facebook.com/millsandboon
- 🅾️ @millsandboonuk
- 🐦 @millsandboon

Or get in touch on 0844 844 1351*

For all the latest titles coming soon,
visit millsandboon.co.uk/nextmonth

*Calls cost 7p per minute plus your phone company's price per
minute access charge

Want even more
ROMANCE?

Join our bookclub today!

'Mills & Boon books, the perfect way to escape for an hour or so.'

Miss W. Dyer

'Excellent service, promptly delivered and very good subscription choices.'

Miss A. Pearson

'You get fantastic special offers and the chance to get books before they hit the shops'

Mrs V. Hall

Visit millsandbook.co.uk/Bookclub and save on brand new books.

MILLS & BOON